One Mile Past
Dangerous Curve

sweetwater fiction

ORIGINALS

TITLES IN THE SERIES:

Greetings from Cutler County: A Novella & Stories
by Travis Mulhauser

How Like an Angel: A Novel
by Jack Driscoll

One Mile Past Dangerous Curve
by Darrell Spencer

One Mile Past Dangerous Curve

a novel

Darrell Spencer

The University of Michigan Press
Ann Arbor

For Kate, as always;
& for Eddie

An excerpt from the novel was published in the *Mid-American Review* under the title *The Devil, You Say*.

This novel is a work of fiction. Names, characters, places, and incidents are either the product of the author's imagination or are used fictitiously. Any resemblance to actual persons, living or dead, to events or to locales is entirely coincidental.

Published in the United States of America by
The University of Michigan Press
Manufactured in the United States of America
∞ Printed on acid-free paper

2008   2007   2006   2005   4   3   2   1

A CIP catalog record for this book is available from the British Library.

Library of Congress Cataloging-in-Publication Data

Spencer, Darrell, 1947–
     One mile past dangerous curve : a novel / Darrell Spencer.
         p. cm. — (Sweetwater fiction. Originals)
     ISBN 0-472-11472-7 (cloth : alk. paper)
     I. Title.   II. Series.

PS3569.P446O54   2005
813'.54—dc22   2004017297

Springtime in Ohio.

Forsythia in bloom, a range of yellow Eddie had not seen except in photographs, butter-cup to pot-of-gold. Daffodils out, urgent and glad-handing. Trees, bushes, shrubs and lawns thirty-seven different shades of green. Tulips in the flower beds the city maintained at intersections, the streets gowned and ready for ballroom dancing. Purple here and there like corsages. Splotches of red and orange foliage. Neon pinks. The maples full of greeting-card blue jays. Woody Woodpeckers hammering tree trunks. Song sparrows chipping in. All of it a pretty to buttonhole you and make you lightheaded and inexact.

Eddie was two thousand miles from his hometown, from Las Vegas, from the clarity of the desert and its thin air, from his daughter, Maggie, from Patty, his ex-wife.

Southeast Ohio, unglaciated, the hindside of the Appalachians, throwback country, five or six letters gone missing from the alphabet here. A place called Athens, two hundred years in the making, and the clay underneath still on the move, shifting in slow-motion and toppling retaining walls when no one was looking. Not a chance in hell any contractor in his right mind

One Mile Past Dangerous Curve   1

was going to insure your basement against leakage. There were steeples and weather vanes, clock towers, Athens Block brick streets and Athens Block brick buildings. Columns, the squared and the round type. Porticos. The old and the new, Colonial in style. A hilly town. Narrow pull-over-and-let-your-neighbor-by roads—mazy, makeshift, stop-gap streets. There was a river, originally the Hockhocking River, but over the years simply Hocking, which right now was five inches from escaping its banks, and the rain was falling, drumming. Thunder cracked, then rollicked through the hollows. Nature letting you know it felt no need to negotiate. The storm could continue, radio was saying, all day, all night. You wouldn't have known drought was on its way, that the summer's corn would be shriveled and ragged, the cucumbers withered skinny runts, and the tomatoes blistered and cracked. Come August, and on-the-spot TV reporters would be interviewing farmers who'd be scratching their heads, who'd be squinting at the heavens, hunkering lackluster to the ground and sifting soil through their fingers. Dirt like their dry breath. There would be threats of rolling brownouts. Then, like the flip of a coin, flash floods, the land too hard to hold the water, wagons found eight miles from their farms, what was left of the crops battered to hell and back, fields of foot-deep swirled mud.

Right this minute it was a downpour in Ohio.

Eddie too often felt turned about here, literally following circles into vertigo and scrambling for landmarks, unable to tell his east from his west, his north from his south. He had tried a compass on a string around his neck, but felt like a schoolboy with a note for the teacher pinned to his shirt. Plenty of hills, but no mountains to orient him. There were too many trees. It was like living in somebody's hair. Joke among Eddie's family was his picture was posted in the hardware stores, employees ordered not sell *This Man* a saw of any kind no matter how he argued or begged.

He sat in his Toyota truck. Close to 180,000 miles on the odometer. Eddie was backed into a slot between stacks of criss-crossed bags of mulch and cords of firewood. *Car Talk* was on the radio, Frick and Frack at the top of their game, Tom and Ray Magliozzi, Click and Clack, the gentlemen who pitched themselves as the Tappet Brothers, some clown saying to them, "When I turn, it's *thank-a, thank-a, thank-a*. It's louder to the right. If I turn right. I turn right and it's THANK-A, THANK-A, THANK-A." Frick repeated what the man said—*Thank-a, thank-a, thank-a*. The doofus said, "It gives me a headache. You know what's causing it?" He played a tape recording of the sound.

Frick said, "You recorded it?"

"I recorded it."

"On a tape recorder?"

"On a tape recorder."

"While you were driving?" Frack said.

"I stuck it out the window."

Frick said, "You were steering? Not the wife? You were at the wheel?"

"Wife left a few years ago."

"This is not hard to believe," Frack said.

"Don't tell me," Frick said, "you were on the Mass Pike?"

"Something like that."

Frick said, "You buy new tires recently?"

Across the parking lot, directly in front of Eddie, was a sign he had begun lettering, a makeshift, poorly nailed-together four-by-eight piece of plywood bolted to shifty four-by-fours. Must have been put in place fifty years ago. The F&G Co-op had hired him to paint it, one of six. All of the signs wobbled or clung to walls by loose screws and nails. Before the rain hit, Eddie laid out and lettered DOW LAKE / PUT AND TAKE. Underneath, LIVE BAIT. Inside the Co-op were earthworms and Day-Glo salmon eggs, which he had seen hand boxed next to the dairy products. He planned to list them and spin a dot alongside each name. Under that, BEER / CIGARETTES / POP. The job meant easy bucks, was mostly repaints, two hours' work, if he could talk the rain into quitting.

Yesterday, Eddie having stopped by, asking did they want any signs done, the manager, restocking those Day-Glo salmon eggs, said, "Bright colors for dumb fish." The man wore a carny barker's mustache and red vest.

Eddie said, "Low IQs on a fish?"

"Trout raised in a hatchery," the man said. "Fish and game people feed them pellets like they was helpless. Then the nimrods dump the whole load in the water, call it 'put and take,' you drop in your line, and it don't matter what you're fishing with or if you don't have a clue, they're on it like sweat."

"So we're talking fish dumb as a lamppost," Eddie said.

"And rubbery to boot. Your dumb, rubbery trout."

"Does anyone show up?"

"Crowds."

Now, waiting on the rain, sitting in his truck, Eddie flicked

4 Darrell Spencer

his lighter. Cut it. Flicked it. *Car Talk* was telling the caller to go out and check his lug nuts, Frick saying, "Don't drive the car," and Frack saying, "You're not on your cell phone, are you?"

Eddie cracked his window and lit a Camel. Frick said to the caller, "Go. Go. Go. Do not pass Go. Do not collect two hundred dollars. Open your trunk and grab your tire iron." Eddie flicked his lighter. Flame. No flame. Flame. No flame. He was asked back in high school what another word for a firebug was, and he said, "Pyromaniac." Answer was ladybug. This in biology class and the asker was Elaine Danzinger, impossible long-legged dream and lab partner aloft on her high stool. Her name followed his in the roll book. Danzinger, but first Eddie Dancer. A name like his belonged on a t-shirt. It was a logo of a name.

Squirrels, close by, did stunts in the trees behind the Co-op. One, on the ground, spotted up like it was settling under a fly ball, then uncoiled itself to its full height, displaying a white underbelly. The squirrel twitched a ragged tail. Had eyes like it was listening to violin. The critter shook and was gone, climbed a tree, trunk to branch to limb, found a telephone cable and hurried along it to a nearby cottonwood. Eddie noticed cardinals. Simple birds, cardinals, particularly the boys. Only bird, an electrician told Eddie, that, one individual sitting alone on a branch, would get in a fight with itself. There was an open field behind the store, and at one end, in a grove of poplars, sat a stubby dew-drop house trailer, Christmas tree lights clipped lazily to it, lit now, it being daylight and the end of April. That was the spirit. On its wooden porch stood a plaster goose wearing a Cleveland Indians baseball cap and a yellow slicker. Next to the trailer was a basketball hoop on a pole, its backboard sawed in half. There was no net, no court but orchard grass and gravel.

Mulch, piled next to Eddie, cost $3.99 a bag. Firewood, $80 a cord. You load. You haul. SPRING ESSENTIALS & SUMMERTIME FUN, a sign said. Eddie's work—twenty-five bucks in his pocket. The rain thinned. It was losing its weight and leaving behind a bluish mist like gun smoke. Next to the sign, lined up and set at an angle to the parking lot in a long low window, were plastic swan planters, side by side, one after the other, forty, fifty of them, like a bad idea breeding on itself.

A silver-haired gent, tight and sleek, six-five, late fifties or early sixties, came out of the Co-op, located Eddie, and trotted over. The crook of his arms said he had played basketball knowledgeably at one time. He hiked his jacket collar against the drizzle and said, "Inside they tell me you're the sign painter."

Eddie said, "When it isn't raining."

The man said, "They say you're good." He was wearing a Southern-lawyer's linen suit, which was beach-sand brown, and he had on two-tone wingtips, chocolate and vanilla. There was something 1940s about him. Natty. He was sporting two thousand dollars worth of haberdashery here in the foothills of the Appalachians, the man thriving and showing off in the wrong time zone. He said, "They're singing your praises."

Eddie, selling himself and his work yesterday, had shown the manager photographs of signs he painted in Las Vegas. The guy offered him twenty bucks worth of snacks for the photograph of a pictorial Eddie painted of Wayne Newton for Caesar's Palace. Original was a big-sucker, square, twenty by twenty feet.

"I appreciate them for that," Eddie said to this gentleman in his clothes.

"You got a card?" the man said and handed Eddie his. *Charles Cotton Investing.* No phone number. No address. Under the name, a *C* joined a *C* like a handshake, and the two letters wrapped around an *I*.

"No card," Eddie said. "Not yet. I can give you a phone number."

"I have some work, if you're interested."

Eddie ripped a piece from the *Athens News* and wrote his number on it.

"I'll telephone," Charles Cotton said. "You seem busy."

Eddie nodded and said, "Late night is good, if you call. After midnight's best."

"I've heard it's best for most things."

Eddie said, "They say it's the time for people of elevated character."

Cotton said, "You don't sleep?"

"In fits and starts."

"Welcome to the club."

Eddie said, "Insomnia?"

"My mind won't shut down," Cotton said.

Eddie said, "I know that story."

Charles nodded, didn't insist on a handshake, and Eddie liked Charles Cotton the way you buddy up to a stranger at a baseball game, to someone you can talk balls and strikes with, to the guy who will go along with your griping about the rule that allows the batter to try to make first base if he swings at a third strike but the ball hits the dirt before the catcher can field it. You and your new pal, you would agree it had something to do with the British and cricket and America's guilt over the Revolutionary War. "Cricket," you would say, "what's with bouncing the ball before the batter hits it?"

Drunk talk. Which could be the best kind. Pals on a footpath.

Charles got into a Lincoln, and Eddie figured he had seen the last of him.

Eddie U-turned in front of Glen and Joy's. His parents' place. Halfway up the driveway was a black BMW, so Eddie parked in the street. Glen was standing in front of Rex Davis, Joy's pastor. He was squared up to Davis, like a boxer cutting off the ring, making it smaller, giving his opponent fewer and fewer escape routes, and Glen was verbally unloading on the man. Eddie's guess was Glen saw Davis drive up, and he charged out of the house to stop the pastor from coming in. The front door was wide open, had been abandoned.

Glen shoved Davis, and Eddie piled out of his truck. He said, "Hey," and hustled across the lawn.

"Bug off," Glen said to him. He jabbed Davis, the pastor fumbling for his car door, Glen so close they seemed hinged. The BMW's engine was running. "No one called you," Glen said to Davis. "We didn't ask you to poke your nose into our family."

Davis said, "Joy phoned my wife, and my wife called me at work."

Glen moved even closer to Davis and said, "Bullshit. End of conversation. Go spit in the ocean."

Davis got the car door open a few inches. Skinny cat might have squeezed through, but not a fat-in-the-butt pastor.

"Beat it," Glen said. "Shoo." He retreated some. To get up a head of steam or let the man go, Eddie wasn't sure.

Eddie said, "What's going on?"

Davis said, "Your mother phoned—"

"My ass and your elbow," Glen said. He outsized Davis by six inches and fifty pounds. Also had forty years on him. But add bluster, and you had real trouble on two legs. "Don't you get it, you SOB?" he said to Davis. "Your phone didn't ring. Get back to your job. Whatever the hell it is you do for the church so you're driving a rich man's car. You work for God and you drive a vehicle costs more than a person's home? How does that happen?"

Davis said, "Joy—"

"Not any God I know," Glen said.

Davis said to Eddie, "My wife said your mother was crying."

"I'm right here," Glen said, and he smacked his own chest. "Don't talk like I'm not big as a horse here in front of you." He slapped his stomach. "What are you?" he said to Davis. "You turn thirty yet? Thirty-five, maybe. You don't know squat, you pip-squeak."

Weak music floated from Davis's car. Flutes. Nervy. Wee folk on woodwinds.

Glen hipped the door shut, saying, "Did you just have your fortieth birthday? Is that why you think you can come to my house and tell me how it is I'm doing? You haven't been on this earth long enough to be coming and telling me that you—or any other shithead on this planet—are worried about how I'm handling things with my wife."

Davis couldn't get past Glen.

Glen said, "I know God."

Davis surrendered. He quit on the door handle.

"Act like a man," Glen said. "You pissant." He had turned an ugly color of gray.

Eddie said, "Glen."

Talking to stone.

He said, "Dad."

Joy, at the front door of the house, clutched the neck of her pink robe. She stepped onto the welcome mat, knowing better than to say one word. She was barefoot. If she coughed, the sky would wobble toward the earth, the ground would turn itself inside out. The foliage, drop its leaves. One more step, and she would be the target.

Glen flung his arm around Eddie's shoulder, gathered him in, and said to Davis, "You're not any older than the boy here, and do you know what the boy knows?"

Eddie wrenched free. Davis didn't move. Eddie ducked past Glen, and Glen grabbed for his arm, saying to him, "Tell Mr. Davis what the boy knows."

Eddie shook Glen off.

"The boy doesn't know squat," Glen said to Davis. "Give the boy a stick, and he'll get hold of the wrong end."

Davis said, "You need help."

Joy withdrew, went back inside the house.

"Tell me what you know," Glen said. "You going to talk to me about a higher power? Did you pray before you hopped in your BMW and came here? Did you talk to God?" Glen stepped onto the lawn, and Davis got his door open. Glen said, "Cancer's got me by the balls. That a problem you can wrap your mind around, Pastor? I did a fast, and I prayed, and the cancer is worse." His eyes got big. Round. Grape-like. He said, "Cancer don't go away. I fasted for three fucking days—you hear me, man of God? X-rays showed the cancer was all through my body." Glen rubbed his face, swiped at his sweaty hair. He said, "God's in his heaven. All's right with the world." He clutched his crotch and said, "Source is right here. You want to lay your hands on me and offer up a prayer?"

Davis started to get into the BMW, and Glen shoved the door into him, said, "Spell Mississippi for us, man of God. Fucking Mississippi. M-i-ss-iss-i-pp-i."

"Sir," Davis said.

"You're not old enough to spell fucking Mississippi."

Davis said, "I'll pray for you."

Glen snatched at him and said, "You'll what?"

Davis put up his hands. He said, "Don't touch me."

Glen said, "You sound like a gasbag. I'm supposed to be the gasbag."

"You're in my prayers."

"My ass," Glen said.

Davis settled into the driver's seat.

"Who combs your hair?" Glen said.

"Maybe," Davis said, "what we need is the cops."

Glen smacked his shoulder. "You calling the cops?" he said. "You little prick."

Davis pulled the door shut and locked it.

"Roll the window down," Glen said. He whacked the glass. Used the butt of his hand. "What kind of man are you?" he said. "You a mouse or a man?"

Eddie positioned himself between Glen and the car. He heard the window zip open, Davis saying, "Your father needs mental help."

The grade-school tattletale. Goody-two-shoes in a suit.

Eddie said to him, "You can see you're making things worse. That's all you're doing here. You're aggravating things. Go, will you? Please."

Davis buzzed his window shut, but didn't seem to want to leave. The engine idled. He had failed. The man of God had not done what a man of God was supposed to do.

Eddie said through the car window, "Get out of here. Drive away."

Glen snorted.

Eddie—now he was yelling—said to Davis, "Are you deaf or just dumb? Get the fuck out of here." He pushed by Glen and went into the house. Left Glen nailed to his spot, Davis backing the BMW out of the driveway. Joy, slumped into a chair, was weeping. She was shaking. "What happened?" Eddie said.

Joy sobbed it out. She was a rag. Glen had come into the

12 Darrell Spencer

bedroom and yelled at her for an hour. The same old story. Who was she seeing? Why didn't she invite her lovers to the house? Bring them to dinner? Who was calling her—all those phone calls? Who was she fucking? He said *fucking* to her. He told her she would be happy when he died, and he loaded one of his guns. He put bullets in slowly, like he was in a gangster movie. Then he took the gun out on the balcony off their bedroom. She came to the door, and he said, "Go see one of your boyfriends." He pointed the gun at her, waggled it, and she called Davis. Got the wife. Joy couldn't even speak. She wept into the phone.

There had been a cave-in, and no way was Joy going to dig herself out. Throw her a shovel, and she'd whack you on the nose with it. She crammed herself lower into the chair. Burrowed in. You could have set her on the curb, pinned a note on her housecoat—*for Goodwill*—said good-bye, and she wouldn't have protested, wouldn't have budged, not even to crawl off. She didn't have the spunk left to care. Her bare feet looked sickly. They had held her upright one day too long.

No Glen out back. Eddie circled the house. No Glen out front.

A sheriff's black cruiser slowed, bumped into the driveway, and Eddie stood by, waiting on the officer. Gold stripes on the side of the car. A big gold star. The man had yanked a small mike from near his shoulder and was talking into it. Then he wrote a note, pulled a hat on, and stepped from his car, saying, "We got a call about an older fellow and a gun."

"The gun's wrong," Eddie said. "The man's my father. He and my mother were arguing."

"I was told there was another man involved."

"A pastor," Eddie said. "My mother called his wife, and he came over." Joy idled near the front door under the porch roof, and Eddie walked the cop to her.

"Ma'am," he said. Actually touched his hat. "You're Mrs. Dancer?"

Joy nodded, and Eddie said to her, "I think the pastor phoned the police."

"My husband's upset is all," Joy said. "He's got cancer—it's killing him, and he gets carried away."

"There was something about a gun?" the cop said.

Joy shook her head. Tears came.

The cop said to Eddie, "Where is your father?"

Eddie told him he was coming out to hunt for him. He was surprised the cop hadn't seen Glen on the streets.

"You say he's not carrying a gun?" the cop said.

"No gun," Eddie said. "He doesn't have a gun on him."

Joy said, "Please bring him home."

Eddie said he could ride along, and the cop said, "That won't be necessary." He handed Joy a card and said, "You need to, you call me." He told them he would drive around, see what he could see. He said, "You call me anytime, Ma'am."

"He's harmless," Joy said.

"He likes to walk in the neighborhood," Eddie said. "He's got a limp, and he's in a jumpsuit. His name is Glen."

`Family shit.`

You begged. You borrowed. You came out the other side. The sun rose, and you put both feet on the floor.

Glen wandered home, and they got through the night, Glen in his La-Z-Boy, the TV loud. Joy upstairs.

Eddie lived to the side of the house in a trailer you couldn't see from the road, at the dead-end of a pea-gravel lane, under a stand of cottonwoods. He chose the place over one of five bedrooms inside. Off his front door, there was a cement patio, a redwood picnic table dead center in the middle of it, a bench on each side. Seven A.M., and he was sitting on top of it. Smoking. Ashtray at his hip. He heard squawks from the television in the house. Its colors reflected in a window. Glen was asleep in the family room off the kitchen, the TV obnoxious. The twentieth century's idea of hearth and fire.

Eddie and Glen, theirs was the old story. Was Act III, The Grudge. At sixteen, the youngest boy, last child of Glen's third marriage, Eddie cut and ran. He backtalked. Going had something to do with tyranny and tyrants and the stomping of a foot. It had to do with the right and wrong way to perform tasks. How you do and do not start a car, open and close a door. What Eddie remembered was Joy coming out to the Mustang he had bought himself, her hairdo as lacy as what you see on a Valentine. She hugged him, kissed his cheek, and Glen appeared. He said, "I got one thing to say. One bit of advice, not that you'll listen. You'll need God in your life."

Now Glen was dying. Eddie's father, seventy-one, more gramps than dad to Eddie. A month ago, Joy phoned, and Eddie came.

To Ohio.

To help Glen, sure, but Joy even more so.

Still, his being here left him feeling the way he always did when someone asked him to look at one of those drawings that flip around on you. Which side of the cube is nearest? Is foregrounded? Is this an etching of a vase? No, it's two people staring at each other. This drawing's of a duck. No, it's a rabbit. The spine of this book is facing out. You lock in on it. It jumps. It's facing in. People got a kick out of them. Foreground, background. Background, foreground. Not Eddie. He wasn't dumb. He got the point. The point pissed him off was all. He hated them the way he hated the Magic Eye in newspapers. Gave him a frigging headache. Some nitpicker's idea of fun.

Eddie lit a Camel off a Camel, felt how he did when he studied that black-and-white photo of a snow-dotted field, the one that asks, *Can you see Jesus's face in this picture?* If you could, you were a believer. If you could not—and Eddie never could—you were a disappointment. You were weak. Your handshake was limp. You had no soul.

Outside McDonald's in Nelsonville one Sunday afternoon, a man pedaling a three-wheeled bike and towing a red wagon full of pop cans had slipped Eddie a flyer. *Hands for Christ,* it said. Bold letters across the top. It told you *How to Make Heaven Your Home* and exhorted you to *Pray this Prayer: Forgive me my sins*.

Put Eddie off his fries, off his cheeseburger.

Sin. There was a concept.

A gigantic cross, on a hill, rising out of the trees, stood above

Nelsonville. You drove by at night and it was lit from underneath. The cross was white. It was very tall and like bone.

Joy was out front gardening. She and Glen owned half an acre here in the heartland, all of it cleared and mowed, their house built against a ridge, into the woods and wildflowers. There was no real back yard. The neighbors behind were higher up and close. Flanking the south side of Glen and Joy's house there was a wooden deck at ground level. A balcony above extended from a third-floor bedroom. North of the yard, a ravine, its belly edge-to-edge trees, collected water and dropped it into the city's drainage.

"Midges?" Eddie said to Joy. He had surprised her. Had come from around the side of the house. She was kneeling next to a square patch of tulips.

"Floaters on my eyes. It's like gnats scooting across them," she said, and she waved at the air in front of her face as if she were fanning herself. She said, "Old age has its blessings."

Joy was talking loud, was trying to be heard over the cicada buzz. Athens was ground zero. The city was hosting the return of a once-every-seventeen-year periodic cicada horde. Estimates put twenty to forty thousand in some trees, one and a half million per acre. Infestation depended on where you lived in the county. The town folk were doing the cicada jitterbug, the old and the young shaking and twisting and swatting. You saw them stomping on the pests and felt the crunch under your own shoe. Joggers dodged them. These runners ducked and swerved and zig-zagged along the roads. During the hottest part of the day there was no holding a conversation outdoors in certain parts of town. The owner of White's Mill advised Joy to cover her young trees and shrubs. He sold her cheesecloth, and Eddie helped her drape what they could reach. The shrubs looked cobwebbed. The smallest trees, cocooned. Under moonlight, the trees, the shrubs, the plants—they stood in the yard like ghosts.

Eddie caught the gloved hand Joy offered him, and he helped her to her feet. She brushed at the grass and dirt on the knees of her pants. Groaned. She said, "The agony and the ecstasy."

Eddie said, "You all set?" He meant for spreading the bags of planting soil stacked in the driveway.

She tapped a spot on the other side of what was left of a cluster of tulips. Stubs now. Deer food. They had bloomed one morning, and by the next day had been nipped clean, their pockets picked, the flowers gone. She said, "Fill all the empty space up to here."

He said, "What are you putting in?"

"Zinnias," she said. She unfolded a sketch she had made of the yard. Areas labeled. *No sun. Sunny, afternoons, late. Morning sun. Black-eyed Susan. Geranium. Peony.* She had laid out a plan for hedges. Juniper and dogwood were supposed to shuttle the deer away from her flowers. Joy was wearing red Top-Siders and was looking cute at sixty-one. Her hair was cut short. She squinted at a tree and said, "If those bugs don't put a sock in it I'm going to cut my ears off."

"I hear they carry away pets and small children," Eddie said.

She said, "They're driving me nuts."

Eddie shoveled and raked, and Joy sat on a plastic footstool. Next to the flower bed she had parked a lawn cart, potted plants in its basket, hand tools in cubbyholes. On the grass, a cultivator and pitchfork.

"You seem to be finding jobs," Joy said.

Eddie poured more soil and said, "You wouldn't say professional signs are a priority around here."

"People do their own is what I'd think."

"Real bad stuff."

"It's what I'd expect," Joy said.

Eddie hoed weeds where Joy had been working and said, "There's a pizza delivery van they've spray-painted the phone number on. Picture them. That ball rattling inside the can, the fools acting like they're using chalk on a blackboard."

"You could see that having a certain kind of appeal these days," Joy said.

"Graffiti?"

"Folksy sells. It stands for independence. People doing things on their own. They're saying they're not going to be hiring someone to do work they can do good enough. They're saying, 'We do it ourselves.'"

"Thus they make good pizza."

"Sure."

"Slogan here seems to be *Will it hold 'til tomorrow?*"

Out near the road, which swung by on the upslope of a steep hill, then curled into a cul-de-sac and dead-ended in front of a local banker's three-story Better-Homes-and-Gardens brick mansion, were dogwoods that had been here long before Joy and Glen bought the house. Their white blossoms, optimistic, had detonated. Under them, Joy had planted wildflowers and was counting the days to their blooming. Neighbors had warned her about one more freeze coming. April, contemplate. May, plant. To the side, on a flat stretch of ground, was a narrow strip of dirt Eddie had tilled and fenced for a garden. Tomato towers were stacked in a corner. No plants here yet. They were inside the mudroom, potted, ready to go. Eddie had dry-stacked flat stones along a flower bed next to the driveway where Joy's garden climbed in tiers like a fortress, honeycombed. More zinnias. Marigolds. A ridge of sweet peas. Eddie saw the flash of a white-tailed deer as it skipped crosswise through the ravine. Then her two babies, the twins, looking over their shoulders. He had seen their beds at the edges of the yard, tall grass packed and swirled. Overhead turkey vultures floated, patrolling the woods. There was no way to scare them off. Boo wouldn't do it.

Glen, semi-retired but antsy as all hell, unable to sit still, had come from Las Vegas to Ohio in February to build and sell Snapper dealerships. Not because he needed money. His strategy was what it had been all his adult life: Hit and run. He arrived, got the businesses going by spring, stuck around through July, maybe August, sold, and returned to Las Vegas. Right now, four buildings were planned, one across the Ohio River, down in West Virginia, a forty-minute drive. Glen and Eddie's stepbrother, Noah, were building one in Nelsonville, fifteen miles north, Glen anticipating where the freeway would eventually bypass the city. They had negotiated one in Lancaster, another hour up 33. Then there was Athens itself. The town was ready for Snapper. Sears had built on Columbus Road. Honda had moved from East State to where an overpass dropped you into the backside of town, the dealership needing room to spread out, Accords on waiting lists, Odysseys on back order, customers standing at the curb ready to drive vehicles away the minute the trucks unloaded them. There was a new national-chain carpet outlet in town. Wal-Mart was coming, if the save-our-way-of-life people didn't win in the courts or burn the building down. Lowe's was on its way. A Staples.

Noah, Glen's son by his first wife, had tagged along. He always did. He had been Glen's partner since Noah was twenty. They came, they built, they sold. Noah rented a house in The Plains and was living with Olive Root, a woman he met when she came to his place to pick up clothes for the Salvation Army. This happened in Las Vegas, Noah winnowing after his second divorce, packing to come to Ohio. He happened to see Olive Root grab a sack he had left in his driveway. Noah forgot to set out the box of boots he meant to donate, so he opened the door and said, "Miss?"

She froze in place, an iron curtain of umbrage taken. Her back to Noah, she said, "Miss?" She whirled and said, "You couldn't be talking to me."

Noah said, "Mrs.?"

She took the boots from him. She said, "Neither."

"Ms.?" Noah followed her to her VW and asked if she would like help getting the door open. She okayed it, dropped in the sack and the box, stuck her hand out, and said, "My name is Olive Root. What's yours, handsome?"

As if life were a screwball comedy. As if the cameras were rolling.

"Noah," he said. He touched the VW's fender and said, "Great toad."

"You mean frog."

There was one painted on the driver's side door. Big. Three feet high. Olive Root had glued a costume jewelry necklace to its throat. The frog's tongue, painted black, curled from its mouth until it stopped at a dent in the back fender where she had written ZAP in gold and added three red exclamation points.

Noah invited her in, and they had coffee, went out to dinner, caught a movie. They dated, and she decided to stay. He welcomed her. Life, Noah told Eddie, had its moments. Two of his sons, the twins, Matthew and Mark, teenagers, fleeing their mother, had moved to Ohio with Noah and Olive Root.

Joy removed her gloves and slapped potting soil and red clay from them. She rubbed her hands together. They were scarred at the wrists, the beauty marks left by surgery for carpal tunnel syndrome. "These hands no longer feel like they belong to me," she once confided to Eddie. Now, here in the yard, she said to him, "My foot did it again." Joy would be driving along, and the toes of her right foot would flop straight down, go stiff and rigid, no rhyme or reason, no warning, and no quick solution. She couldn't force or will them into place. She had to pull over, take off her shoe and massage each toe until, one by one, they relaxed. Big toe first, she had figured out.

"It worries me," Eddie said.

Joy said, "It worries you? It scares the living daylights out of

22 Darrell Spencer

me." She rubbed her wrist and said, "One second I'm fine. Then away they go, and by the time they're normal again I'm ready for the loony bin."

"Should you be driving?"

"I'm not giving up driving," she said. She waved at the world and all its niggling injustices. She wasn't a whiner. She understood how day by day life meant diminished expectations. No thumb in the dike was going to hold back time. She said, "Thank God for driving."

Glen appeared on the third-floor balcony, facing the ravine. He stared down at them. Didn't wave. What a ball of wax the man was.

Eddie said, "Why don't you guys go back to Las Vegas?" What he didn't say was, *So Glen can die in peace.*

Joy said, "You know how they say somebody's heart is in the right place?"

"Sure."

"His isn't. His took a U-turn."

Exactly.

They heard a honk. Mark and Matthew pulled to the curb in front of the house. The boys were driving Olive Root's VW, had been the ones who insisted on driving it across the country. They loved the frog, the car's color, its retro-sixtiesness. The VW was so uncool it was cool. Joy waved them into the driveway. She had hired them to clean the rain gutters. The ones on the south side of the house had grass growing in them. You could see it from the yard.

First Matthew, then Mark, hugged Joy. Their gram. They said *Hey* to Eddie, who was thinking they had grown six inches

One Mile Past Dangerous Curve   23

since he last saw them. Had to be over six feet tall now, and they were the gangly you see in distance runners. Long arms. Big hands and thick elbows, like they had plenty of growing yet to do. They had begun to do things with their hair. Spike it. Color it. Mark's had a blueness to it. Matthew's was gold. Piercings were around the corner.

"Put us to work," Mark said.

Matthew said, "You need your house moved a foot to the left or the right, we can do that." The kid had a smile on him.

"Another time," Joy said. "Today it's rain gutters."

Eddie didn't really know the twins. These were Noah's gifted children. Truly gifted. Certified gifted. Their mother had collected about two hundred test scores to prove it.

Bright kids answer questions correctly. Gifted kids turn answers into questions.

Bright kids pay attention. Gifted kids would like to, but it's all so boring, and they already know what you're getting at.

The world wants the end product. Solutions. Gifted kids revel in process. Enjoy being off-balance.

Bright kids solve math problems. Gifted kids play with math.

Whatever checklist you used, Matthew and Mark came up gifted. At age four, they read novels. At six, they wrote them, the kind that invited you to choose your own path through the book and then select from among alternate endings. They put together pop-up books. At Joy's one night, years ago, Eddie saw a video of the two of them—they looked to be about ten— sitting on a leather couch, debating about a *Time* magazine article on trade deficits. Noah's first wife, Angie, kept portfolios of their grades, their drawings, the letters they wrote to presidents

24 Darrell Spencer

and legislators. Her claim was that she spotted their genius when they were two days old. Her goal, from that minute on, was to spend her life nurturing it and documenting it. She had a camera rolling the day Mark walked up to Matthew and said, "Did we as human beings discover numbers or did we make them up?"

Her boys mastered the usual musical instruments—the trumpet, the guitar, the piano. It was Matthew who discovered the vibraphone. Mark countered with a flügelhorn.

One of their grade-school teachers asked the students in her class to name everything they could think of that was square. First words out of Mark's mouth were, "Mr. Rogers and his neighborhood." And Matthew added, "Johnny Carson and his sidekick, Ed." Then the two of them cut square shapes into pieces of paper and walked around framing objects in the room. Angie had the teacher write down everything the woman could remember—what Matthew and Mark said, how they acted, how the kids reacted, how they talked to the other children.

It was Angie's out of control meddling that sent the twins off to Ohio with Noah and Olive Root. She didn't talk to Matthew and Mark; she empowered them. They didn't go on trips; they went on outings. The boys wanted to mow the lawn and not have their doing it turn into a lesson in geometry. So they begged and quarreled and reasoned—wrote briefs—and fought until Angie relented. The three of them struck a bargain, cut a deal. Matthew and Mark would attend Fordham Academy the summer after graduation, then go on to Yale, if they could first go to a regular high school in Ohio. One year, that was all they were asking for.

Joy loved the twins.

Both of them insisted on shaking Eddie's hand, an act he hated in general and even more so in the particular, his theory being *who knew where that hand had been?*

Joy asked Eddie to help them haul the ladders out of the garage. They set up, and Eddie told them he would tell Glen what the boys were doing. "Better safe than sorry," Eddie said, the three of them standing at the foot of two ladders side by side, a few feet apart. "He might be thinking you're breaking in. He likes to wave a pistol around."

The boys looked puzzled.

"I think I'm joking," Eddie said, "but I'm not sure."

Matthew said, "He's dying."

"He's got cancer," Eddie said. They knew that. Eddie said, "It's too late to do anything about it."

"Noah told us," they said. Then, as if on cue, they said, "We're looking for turtles."

Eddie said, "Turtles?"

"Chelonians," Mark said.

Matthew said, "You seen any around?" Joy had walked over. He looked to her.

Joy glanced at Eddie.

Mark said, "Mostly box turtles."

Matthew said, "Genus *Terrapene*."

"You know what's cool," Mark said, "they can live over a hundred years. They've been found with initials in their shells from farm people who lived in the 1800s."

Matthew said, "We're thinking of ranching them."

Eddie said, "Ranching them?"

26   Darrell Spencer

"It's a radical new idea," Mark said.

Joy said, "You boys leave the turtles alone." She started toward the house, saying, so the words floated along with her, "Do the gutters and let the wildlife be."

They turned to Eddie. He shrugged and said he would be around back if they needed anything.

"Ranching's the best of both worlds," Mark said. "We get rich, the turtles get a free ride."

Eddie said, "Keep an eye out for Glen. You see him out on the balcony, make sure he knows who you are."

The boys each had one foot on a ladder.

Eddie said, "You're okay. He's sad, but not insane."

Cotton did phone, and the next day Eddie followed Cotton's directions out the backside of Athens and under the freeway that took you to Columbus. He stayed with 550 as if he were driving to Amesville, but turned left on Alderman, which you missed if your thoughts were on pleasure rather than business, and then Eddie took a quick-and-hurried right at the Augustine Cemetery, and he was on Liar's Corner Road. Near most of the tombstones were American flags. Row after row. It was a celebration of some kind. Easter? Flags for Christ? That made no sense. Downtown one day, Eddie noticed a bumper sticker on a car. *Christ Is Coming. Look Busy.* Last weekend, he stopped at the K-Mart at the far end of East State, and a woman standing at the entrance asked him if he wanted a palm leaf. Eddie told her he was only passing through, and she said, "It's the human condition, honey, all of us like ships sailing by." She said, "Take one, honey." So he did, and it hit him. It was Palm Sunday—Christ, a donkey, the ride into Jerusalem, palm leaves laid under hoof and foot.

Religion in the heartland—it wasn't about to let you forget it.

What had Glen said all those years ago? You'll need God in your life.

Liar's Corner road dipped and doodled and carried you through woods and posted land. Eddie was to look for a gate on the right side little more than a mile up. Set your odometer, Cotton had told him. Cock your hat. The gate would be that silver you see on water tanks. Most of the homes Eddie saw were trailers yanked into hillsides or anchored slantwise on the top of ridges. Three or four jammed together. Everyone owned a dog tied to a doghouse or barking from a chainlink pen. One place had what looked like a dozen—rottweilers, labs, coon hounds, one cocker whose coat was matted into dreadlocks. Each had its own igloo-looking hut lined up like barracks.

Yard art at every bend. Front yards, side yards, back yards. Gazing balls, concrete squirrels, and white-tailed deer. Plaster Christs, arms open, welcoming. Salvation. Mother Marys, hands cupped in front. All of it laid out to some purpose, to ward off whatever it was that had to be warded off. It was the work of people with too much time on their hands, was the mischief done by people who didn't have easy access to medications. Was worthy of misdemeanor charges. There were pink flamingos whose wings twirled in the breeze. There were plaster geese and ducks dressed in clothes. One in a yellow slicker.

28   Darrell Spencer

One in a Quaker cloak. There was one in cap and gown. Eddie stopped to read a short piece of two-by-four nailed to a tree, *Here is Here* scribbled on it. The road was do-si-do if anyone came the other way. Hillocked. Humped deeply. He nearly high-centered at the bottom of a hollow. Left, right, behind, ahead, nothing but trees. The sky, where had it gone? It was lost, but for a sliver at the top of the bend and some shuddering of sunlight on the hood of Eddie's truck.

Cotton was sitting on top of the gate, talking into a cell phone. He hopped off and signaled Eddie through. He relooped and locked a chain. He walked alongside Eddie's car, escorting him deeper into the woods on a gravel and grass road, which, up a hill and around a switchback, dropped steeply left and opened onto a field and a ranch house. No way would you have believed the place was out here if you hadn't seen it. The house was long and low. It sat on acres of mowed grass, and there was a pond—dock, rowboat, swans. Come evening, no doubt you would hear the bullfrogs, their calling of the roll, their orchestrated sorrow. Eddie parked, and Cotton, who had hustled inside the house, returned carrying Rolling Rock, two bottles, ice-cold.

Eddie commented on the solitude, the quiet, and Cotton said, "You can't beat it, but for the occasional automatic-weapon fire you hear some nights, late."

Man was kidding, right?

"You know, that distinct sound," Cotton said, and he mimicked it.

Eddie said, "You're not joking."

"No one around here is," Cotton said. "The hills are alive."

One Mile Past Dangerous Curve   29

"You'd think a rifle, maybe. Something like that."

"We're not talking legal."

Eddie said, "It's so pretty. You'd think—" He stopped before stupid—capital S—dropped from his mouth. What did pretty have to do with fools and guns?

Eddie and Cotton dragged together a couple of butterfly chairs on the porch, which sat high off the ground, six steps up, and Cotton told Eddie that the job was twenty signs, and there might be more. Could be as many as fifty.

"What size?" Eddie said. "Big? Small?"

Cotton said, "To go by the side of the road."

"Four by eight?"

"Four by eight feet?" Cotton stretched his arms wide, trying to imagine the size. He said, "That sounds good."

Eddie said, "Are we talking two-lanes? Little roads? Highway? Interstate?"

"Good roads, but not major ones. The ones that get you from here to there in the countryside."

"Four by eight will be good, then. Four by eight is what you use for that kind of sign."

"You're the boss."

"You want a bid, I'll need details," Eddie said.

"Job is yours, if you're okay with it," Cotton said.

He wrote out his first one on the back of one of his cards. It said, CAN'T SLEEP? TRY TALKING TO THE SHEPHERD RATHER THAN COUNTING SHEEP.

Eddie asked Cotton if he was a born-again, and Cotton said, "Six or seven times over but not in the way you mean."

"They'll all be religious?" Eddie said.

30   Darrell Spencer

Cotton said, "Not always."

"You a preacher?"

"You know how they say something is so far to the opposite of something else that it becomes the thing it's the far side of?"

Eddie took a swig. "Too deep for me," he said.

"You take sadness as far as you can to the extreme, and it becomes happiness." Cotton was in short sleeves. On his forearm was a crude tattoo of a skull and crossbones. Looked like it had been drawn by a child, and the ink had bled the way ink does on a blotter. Under the bones was the number 13. Ugly figures. He drank Rolling Rock and said, "That's the way it is with me and preachers. I'm so far the other way that I am one."

Eddie saluted him with his beer. He said, "There you go."

The first letter of each sign was to be fancy, the way you see, Cotton explained to Eddie, in old books. "Illuminated manuscripts?" he said. "Is that the name I'm looking for?" He waggled his beer. It was close to empty. He said, "Medieval. Something like that. The Bible. What monks did all day long. You know what I'm saying? What I'm asking for?"

Eddie said, "Fancy can be unreadable on a sign if you're driving by and going somewhere."

"Think like Route 56. You driven it?"

"Several times."

"Say you're headed to Circleville. Think about the drive there, and you'll have in mind what I mean."

"Sure. Got it."

Cotton said, "Another beer?"

Eddie shook his bottle. "Better not."

"You a believer?" Cotton said.

One Mile Past Dangerous Curve   **31**

Eddie said, "Do I have to be?"

"For the job, no." Cotton slugged the last of his Rolling Rock and said, "Your work is professional. That's what I'm after. I want signs that say they're to be taken seriously. That get respect. No one dashed them off. We want signs that'll stop people in their tracks."

"We?"

"Me. You. We. Us." Cotton fiddled with his bottle, thumb-popping its mouth. Making music. He said, "I'm not a believer. This is personal."

Eddie said, "Do you want me to put them in the ground?"

"I got that covered."

"Where do they go?"

"Here and about. I'll take care of that end of things."

"It's a practical question," Eddie said. "How far the sign is from the cars makes a difference in letter size and style. It can affect what colors I use, the layout."

"Undetermined exactly where right now," Cotton said. "But close to the road, so they're there where, say you're going over the river and through the woods to grandmother's house, the signs become a presence big enough you'll brake and get out of your car. Maybe you'll snap a picture."

Eddie asked if Cotton had permits. He said, "It's the law most places."

"That's covered too."

Eddie estimated a price for the one sign, and Cotton said he would pay all of it in advance. "Twenty times that?" he said.

"One at a time," Eddie said. "They could cost different. Cheaper. Maybe more. Because of color, the design and layout.

A can of paint can vary twenty dollars in price."

Cotton gave Eddie cash in an envelope, and they walked toward his truck. "You tell people you're working for me, you'll hear that I murdered my wife," Cotton said.

Eddie thought on that. He said, "Is that an expression around here? Like someone saying, 'You work for me, you'll hear I'm a hard-ass'?" Eddie opened the Toyota's door.

"It's not just an expression. It's a rumor," Cotton said. "Will it bother you?"

"If you killed your wife?"

"If you hear talk that I did."

A woman inside the house walked past the window behind where they had been sitting. Her dark hair was cut short.

Eddie said, "People beat their gums too much."

"You're a diplomat," Cotton said.

"I don't think so," Eddie said. "You murdered someone I figure you'd be in jail or run out of town. I could be mistaken. It seems like what goes on in these hollows is kept in the family. One of those eye-for-an-eye places. Vengeance left in the hands of the folks who need to take it. I'm not from here." He thought about the trailers and houses he had passed. *No Trespassing. Stay Off. There's a phone in town. They'll let You Use it.* Eddie ducked into his truck and said, "I'll get that first one done and you see what you think. We'll go from there."

The woman who had cruised by the window cracked the storm door and said, "Charles, there's a call."

Cotton held up his cell phone for her to see. He said, "Give them this number," and the woman shut the door. Cotton trailed Eddie down the lane, his phone ringing.

One Mile Past Dangerous Curve   **33**

Rain, thunder, sun. More rain. The proverbial buckets. An Ohio morning. Thunder like a mule. Big drops of water thumping the ground. Lightning. All of it, backstage sound effects.

Eddie opened the trailer's front door. At nine, there had been another UPS delivery. Always they were for Glen. From Us-to-You Videos, movies like *Backside Babes in the Woods*. *Pair-o-Dice*. Handling instructions said, TAKE AROUND SIDE TO TRAILER.

And here was Glen to collect his porn. He was soaked. "This is something. Mother Nature crying to beat the band," he said. He shook his head at the storm, arms outstretched. Eddie found him a towel, and Glen dried off. He was carrying a butter knife he was using to slice open the day's mail he had collected from the box out by the road. He handed Eddie a thick manila envelope from Maggie. Eddie opened it and took a quick look. There were photos, a Post-it attached to one: *Eddie, grow up. Get a computer. We can chat. I can send pictures. Plug in, Eddie. Plug in.* Her letter was long. He shuffled through it. On the last page, she had written vocabulary words. Maggie's to learn, but she wanted her dad speaking the same language, so he was to look them up and do his homework. Yes, there would be a quiz. Last week's words were *churlish, punctilious, cozen, intractable*. And, *fug*. Eddie's daughter was coming to terms with the world. She included a few of her drawings. Eddie set the letter aside. He didn't want Glen around when he read it. He didn't want to show the old guy the photos and the drawings.

Glen skimmed a letter he had cut open, then handed it to Eddie and said, "Here's one answer to all your troubles." WHO OWNS YOU? the junk mail asked at the top. It was addressed to Glen. First line said, *Do you own your future—or do THEY?* All in bold print. *You* and *they* underlined in red.

Glen said to Eddie, "You seen your mother?"

"She's gone somewhere," Eddie said. "I saw her driving off."

"I figured. Car's gone." Glen cut a letter open and said, "Was she dolled up?"

"I couldn't see."

Glen was wearing a jumpsuit and slip-on house shoes. *IMAGINE*, the junk mail said. *IMAGINE IF one day in the near future you were informed that over HALF of your paycheck could be confiscated to support a large, affluent, politically powerful group of people* who do not work at all . . .

Eddie sat and punched on ESPN. He muted the sound.

"Judas Priest," Glen said. He flashed another letter at Eddie and read out loud its salutation: "Dear Senior Citizen." He took a seat in close to Eddie and said, "Why don't they be honest and just say it? Spell it out. Put *old fart* there in print. Dear Old Fart."

Eddie was reading the first letter. *IMAGINE IF*, it said, *one morning you awakened to discover that the horror of drug violence in America had become just a memory, like the gangster mayhem of the Prohibition era* . . .

IMAGINE. And again, *IMAGINE*.

Then the letter asked, *Sound intriguing?*

If the junk mail was right about Glen, if it was right about

One Mile Past Dangerous Curve   35

him, if it knew what kind of sound-thinking, hardworking American Glen was, the junk mail was betting Glen would say *YES* to *Reason,* the magazine for people who want to know what there is to know about today's issues. If *Reason* was right about Glen, Glen would detach the token and insert it where it said, *INSERT TOKEN HERE.* Glen would say, *YES.* Glen would say, *SEND MY FREE ISSUE.* And if he was disappointed (if the junk mail knew Glen, he wouldn't be), Glen could simply write *CANCEL* on the invoice and return it. The free issue of *Reason* was Glen's to keep, and he would owe *Reason* nothing.

IMAGINE THAT.

"Lights above the trees woke me last night," Glen said. "About two in the morning." He waved an envelope toward the ceiling. Aimed skyward and said, "Say what you want, this was no ordinary airship, and it was egg-shaped. If I was a guessing man, I'd say I was probably seeing running lights."

Eddie said, "Probably kitchen in the house on the ridge above us."

"Ezekiel saw them," Glen said. "Read your Bible."

Glen was following in his own father's footsteps, was taking Mr. Highway's path. What Eddie knew about his grandfather, what he understood about Mr. Highway, amounted to next to zip, only that sometime in the late 1930s the man made a million off cattle in Wyoming, discovered the highway to Salt Lake City, Utah, where he invested in hard-rubber tires and lost the million, then skidded onto another highway, one that wove south along the foothills of the Wasatch Mountains, and stopped in a farm town called Spanish Fork, where he grew apples, until he heard about a highway winding its lonely-ass

36   Darrell Spencer

way into southern California. Next was a two-lane cutting through the Mojave Desert to Arizona. Then there was the Great Basin and a road into Nevada. Clara, Mr. Highway's wife, Glen's mother, Eddie's grandmother, tucked their nine children into her pockets and a handbag, and, her finger waves fading to gray and weakening year by year, she tagged along. Running out of piss, vinegar, and hope the family landed in Ely, Nevada, Mr. Highway riding the backcountry for the national parks people. One winter morning he asked Glen and another son, Art, to put on their long pants, get serious work, or strike out on their own. Mr. Highway wasn't bringing in nearly enough food or money to feed and clothe eleven people, and Glen and Art were the oldest. Glen seventeen. Art eighteen. There was no work to be had in Ely, so Glen did construction over near Reno and into California and finally rode a bus to Las Vegas where he apprenticed himself to a bricklayer named McIffen. Glen completed college on the sly and was graduated a certified public accountant. He got into franchising, McDonald's, Kentucky Fried Chicken, Snapper, and he paid nickels for land in Paradise Valley which he sold for dollars as the city spread its tacky self toward the mountains on all sides. Glen took a pledge: one life, one town, one house. Which he broke, over and over and over again. Which he hadn't kept except in principle. He owned a place in Las Vegas he refused to sell. Eddie grew up in San Diego, Tucson, Phoenix, Sacramento, Denver, Portland, and Butte, Montana.

Thus Ohio, where, like Mr. Highway, Glen was franchising and seeing UFOs. Mr. Highway had encountered aliens in Wyoming. They rustled his cattle. You blinked your eyes,

Glen had told Eddie, and they were gone, the ships and your herd.

Glen stacked the letters into two piles. Bills, Joy's job. Junk, his to trash.

"This morning, I'm out early—fog, but no rain yet, and I'm walking when I run into the lady up the street," Glen said. "I'm out there doing my old-fart dance-of-death up and down the streets, getting the blood pumping, doing my constitutional. I had a tune in my head and I was whistling it when I heard a voice say, 'Just the other day I was standing in the post office and I was saying, *What's happened to all the whistling men?*'" It was the woman who lived around the bend near the church, and she was speaking to Glen. He hadn't noticed her. Had walked right past. But there she was big as life on her lawn. You saw her, in daylight, at night, in the rain, in the snow, hell or high water, and you thought the world had gone to pot. It was six-thirty in the morning, and she was yakking at Glen from her yard. She had smeared her lipstick all over her chin and her cheeks. It was some kind of orange smudge. Her hair was a dishcloth. It was the color of mud and tossed on top of her head.

Glen, sitting here with Eddie, Glen in full barfly posture, zipped his jumpsuit to his throat. He popped his lips. He said, "Most of the world is sick, you know that's a given. That woman is cheap, her hair and her. What you see is what you get, huh?"

Eddie said, "So what you're telling me is that you and Joy won't be inviting her to dinner any time soon." He placed the

Reason letter on Glen's junk pile. ESPN was hustling through highlights of the NBA playoffs.

Glen said, "She says what she said about whistling men, and I'm searching her bushes with my eyes, afraid this is a setup so early in the day, and I'm going to be clubbed." He was thinking she was slowing him down so her pals could mug him. Ohio was a different kind of place. People in Las Vegas, they didn't flag you down and talk to you out of the blue. They didn't bother you like she was, like this crazy lady was doing. A pretty like this Ohio could confuse you into letting your guard down. You could be tricked. You know the way the woman does the hitchhiking when there's also some birdbrain and a dog, so the birdbrain and the dog hide off in some bushes and they're fooling you into stopping. The woman showing some leg. You slow, and out they come, running. Glen got to thinking this situation with this lady was like that. He was walking in the middle of the street, and she was mouthing off from her yard where she was doing something in the flowers. She had dirt on her. There could have been someone else, some loser hiding there in her yard. Glen said to her, "Was I whistling?" He told Eddie he was twisting his head sideways the way old coots do when they look at you. He said to Eddie, "You notice that, how we do it? Like a brick could come hurling at us from any direction."

"I've missed it," Eddie said. He was focused on ESPN.

"It's a treat. Watch for it."

"I'll keep my eyes open."

"This woman, she says to me, 'You were. You were whistling like a songbird.' I thanked her, but I'm not stupid. I'm endowed with brains. When I was a kid, wherever I was with my mother, she said to anyone who stopped long enough to listen, 'We've got a smart one on our hands. Maybe too smart, too smart for his own britches.'" Glen leaned back, sat like an open cupboard door. He realigned his letters, shifted his box of videos, and started reciting. He said, "*I took a contract to bury the body / of blasphemous Bill MacKie. / Whenever, wherever or whatsoever / the manner of death he die—Whether he die in the light o' day / or under a peaked-faced moon.*"

Dangerous Dan McGrew.

Glen knew it by heart. Had learned it as a schoolboy.

Casey at the Bat.

The Ballad of Salvation Bill.

The Spell of the Yukon.

Eddie grew up with all of them. Anywhere, anytime, Glen breaking into poetry. Or song. Bing Crosby's stuff.

"Word for word," Glen said. "Still, at my age." He commenced reciting. Said, "*I wanted gold, and I sought it / I scrabbled and mucked like a slave.*"

Eddie said, "You got a mind like flypaper. What hits it sticks."

"I sang for pay in high school," Glen said. "I was a balladeer, a crooner. But not now. This crazy woman, she thinks she's fooling me, but she isn't. You flatter some old fool who's out walking the streets and you've got something up your sleeve. My whistling, it's a penny whistle if it's anything."

Eddie stood up, ready. At attention here in the world. The storm had stopped. He had a sign to do. He had places to go. There were hands to shake and babies to kiss.

Glen didn't budge. The man had assembled to his shoulders and arms enough melancholy to knock good cheer sideways. Life was picking on him. Was harrowing Glen beyond any purgatory he had ever imagined. He brought his feet together so that they looked crippled, as if another disease, say polio, after all these years, had finally gotten a grip. He acted like he might fold in on himself. He said, "Boy, the doctors took my manhood."

Eddie sat down. He punched off the TV.

Glen said, "No one should be allowed to do that to people."

Behind Huntington Bark, in the window of the cafe where he and Eddie had come, two-foot-high red neon said EAT. Outside, near the highway, was a repaint Eddie had done. His pay was breakfast for two weeks. Extra rolls. The sign said *Roy's. Truckers Welcome. Open 24 Hours.* It stood by the two-lane to Columbus, which was thirty feet from the cafe across the dirt parking lot. Eddie had called Huntington about some sign work. Traffic on 33 zipped past. There was a semi parked out front, its cab popped open like the lid to a cigarette lighter.

Huntington was telling Eddie that the way he heard it was that Charles Cotton came to teach at the university in the late sixties. Only his name wasn't Cotton back then. Athens was the man's hometown, and he was returning. He had that year graduated from the University of West Virginia. He comes, and the woman with him, it's taken for granted, is his wife. She's a honey. And he doesn't disabuse anybody of their notions about her. Then months later a pregnant woman arrives on a bus, lady white as a piece of typing paper, copper hair put together like a country singer's. It's got height. She's got a face full of freckles. She's around town one day asking for Cotton by name. Only Cotton isn't the name she's using. It's a French-sounding name she's saying. Le something. Short. Like LeGoff. And the given name is common, is one you think of when you think of French names. Jacques, something like that. Or Marc, you know, with a *c*. It's a name Huntington can't recall, though he's privy to it, though privy seems not quite the way to say what he feels but is the sense he has of the name floating loose in the back of his head. He'll ask around, he tells Eddie. This woman hauls out a photo everywhere she goes. It's of her and Cotton, if Cotton is the guy. This is thirty-five years ago, back when Huntington was a kid. Of course it turns out this pregnant lady, she's the real wife. She has been twiddling her thumbs over in Pennsylvania, waiting for Cotton—again, if it is Cotton—to come for her. He's getting settled, he's told her. He's hunting lodging, he writes to her. Fibs. Nothing but a pack of lies. *We'll need room*, he says. Baby on its way and all. He hopes she understands that what he's doing isn't easy. It's not a cakewalk. Two months she waits. No fetching occurs. She is carrying postcards when she shows up. She passes them around. *Wish you were here. Got a lead on a place.* They're all signed by the French-sounding name. Jacques. Or Marc. LeGoff. Huntington is pretty sure he's right about the surname. LeGoff. One postcard says, *Hot and humid. Whew.* So she comes on her own, all noise and ripe, traipsing up and down Court Street, hauling herself and her belly here and there. She learns he's got a house out near what

42   Darrell Spencer

is now, but wasn't then, Fox Lake. Someone offers her a ride, out of kindness and curiosity. There's a reunion of sorts in front of whoever it was who drove her to the professor's. Then good-byes, and the professor gets her alone and he kills her, stuffs her in an oil drum, and here Huntington is missing the details (like, where is the other woman in all this?), but the professor is caught out at Dow Lake where he's gone to hide what he's done. There are bullet holes in the oil drum. Eventful trial follows. Covered statewide. Crowds at dawn at the courthouse, sack lunches in hot hands. The professor is convicted, sent to prison in northeastern Ohio, where his dad, who has only within the last year gotten out of the clink himself, helps Cotton escape, and neither one of them is recaptured. Ever. An unlikely story, but true as a plumb line. The facts are available to anyone who asks.

Huntington will get the professor's name. LeGoff, Cotton, whoever it was, he grew up here, before he went away and then came back to teach. Before he killed his wife. "But," Huntington said to Eddie, "it would be that French name. Of course, he would have changed the name. You'd choose a name like Cotton. After he got away, he'd get a new one. He'd be stupid to come back at all. What for? What would be the point? A man cold-blooded enough to kill a pregnant lady, his own wife and kid, does he need to take the risk? Get in people's faces?"

"Maybe he wants to say he's sorry?" Eddie said.

Huntington said, "There's a thought." He buttered toast. He said, "On the other hand, a man with that kind of meanness in him, he might enjoy throwing it all up in our faces."

Eddie said, "After so many years?"

One Mile Past Dangerous Curve   43

Huntington said, "Maybe he found Christ."

"So," Eddie said, "he's making up for what he did."

Huntington said, "How would him coming here and buying himself a rich house out in the hills be equal to him making up for killing his wife? What kind of logic is at work in that?"

Good question.

But then *how* would you make up for doing what the professor had done? In a million years, how would you pay for killing your wife and your unborn child?

Logic was out the door with the bathwater.

"You ask around, you'll get an earful," Huntington said. "The lawyer who defended the murdering professor is alive and kicking. He's heavier and less mobile than he was, and profoundly forlorn the later you talk to him in the day, but able to stand with the help of a cane, and he will cut loose with the words. People who were teenagers will tell you stories. Hell, there are adults around who can fill in all the details, townspeople who showed up at the courthouse at six in the morning to get a seat. It was a big deal."

Eddie said, "So who's the woman?"

Huntingon said, "The one he brought with him, the one everybody was thinking was the wife?"

"No. The one at Cotton's place now."

"She young?"

Eddie said, "I only saw her for a second."

"He's introducing a young lady as his daughter," Huntington said.

Eddie said, "What's your take on it?"

Huntington creamed his coffee. He stirred it, sipped. He was studying on his take. He didn't, so it seemed in the end, have one. He showed with his two hands how he regretted the poverty of his thought. He said, "It's something to talk about, is all."

Eddie said, "You mean the woman?"

"I mean the murder. Who he is."

Eddie said, "Wouldn't some of those townspeople be able to recognize whether it was him or not?"

Huntington shrugged. He said, "One day I'm eating lunch right here, one of those tables over there, and a woman comes in. I don't pay any attention at all. Then I see she's staring at me. We're close enough we can talk. I drink my coffee. I eat my eggs. Then I hear her say, 'You got no idea who I am, do you?' I didn't. It turns out she was a girl I knew in high school. She was a girl I'd spent a few months screwing."

"Did you recognize her when she told you who she was?"

"I wouldn't have," Huntington said. "Not if you threatened to remove my spleen. I acted like I did. To be nice, but I'm betting she saw through that. She knew I didn't recognize her." He drank coffee and said, "People change so you don't know who they are. Twenty years, thirty years. It's like they become someone else, and I mean physically."

Eddie said, "I guess."

"Go to your high-school reunion," Huntington said. "You'll see."

"Sure," Eddie said. "I bet you're right."

So it was back to their business, Eddie subcontracting a sign to Huntington, one for the new Days Inn. Could Huntington build it by Saturday? No problem. Get it in the ground? Yes, sir. There was also some work for Big Bear, the grocery store, and a billboard for Glen and Noah's Snapper franchise in Nelsonville. Eddie was painting a banner for a supper club and needed someone to hang it. Huntington was the man. He drove a cab part-time in the summer, full-time come winter. He lived in a trailer at the Lake Snowden Campground. Had a cat named Chester and a woman in town he lived with when the subzeros hit. She couldn't stand the trailer. Huntington mowed lawns, did cement work, could roof a house, and he changed your heater filters for a couple of bucks. He did grouting and laid tile. He appreciated highjinks and fast cars. It was his dad who named him Huntington. The counterweight, the man said, to hanging the last name of Bark on him. In the fall, Huntington raked and bagged leaves and cleared rain gutters. He told Eddie, "They say you give Huntington Bark something round and he'll make it rounder."

"Rounder, huh," Eddie said.

"I'm the man," Huntington said, "can show you the difference between a left-handed and a right-handed screwdriver."

On the phone, sitting on the redwood table, Eddie told his exwife, told Patty, that the murdering professor was going to sink the body in Dow Lake. Why else the holes?

Patty wondered if the wife was dead first.

Eddie hadn't asked. "She'd have to be," Eddie said. "Otherwise she'd be inside kicking and screaming for all she was worth."

"You work for this guy?" Patty said.

Eddie said, "It's gossip, is all. What are the odds?"

46 Darrell Spencer

"You know what they say about an ounce of truth."

Eddie had called to talk to Maggie, a.k.a. M&M since she was five, because of Patty's calling her Mad Maggie or Majestic Maggie, nicknames determined by the turn their daughter's heart took at dawn, by which side of the bed she crawled out of, the angry side or the sunshine-in-your-heart side. The girl was fifteen now. Eddie had phoned at the wrong time. Maggie was sleeping over at a friend's. He had worked up descriptions of Ohio he wanted to try out on his daughter. She loved it when he got into what she called his kiss-and-tell mode, when he opened up and rolled out the details, and she would say, "You're flying by the seat of your pants, Eddie." Or, "No way, Eddie-o. You're letting loose the lions of your imagination." The kid floored Eddie day after day, year after year, minute to minute. Who would have thought his girl could be such a fancy dancer—either small *d* or capital *D*? He planned to tell her how the deer knocked on his door this morning—rap, rap, rap— and asked to borrow a cup of sugar, the mother and her twins, white tails, spots like sunlit coins on their sides. He would describe last night's possum sitting in the tree like Alice's Cheshire Cat. The creature winked at Eddie. No lie. It looked like it was wearing a cheap toupee. Mostly there was Roscoe the toad to tell her about. Nights, late, Eddie sat on the top of this redwood table and sucked on a Camel, and there, right next to him, was Roscoe, hunkered upon himself, crouched, not more than a foot from Eddie. A narrow white stripe curved down the toad's back, dark symmetrical spots flanking it. Roscoe had hooded eyes, and he was as calm as a monk. Had the presence of a paperweight.

One Mile Past Dangerous Curve   47

"We talk," Eddie had planned to tell M&M. "Me and Roscoe."

She would say, "Heavy subjects?"

He would say, "How hilarious math can be."

"Yeah?"

"What toads watch on television."

M&M would say, "Eddie, it sounds to me like you're at the weed again. You're off the wagon."

"You know it's BS," Patty said to him about Cotton. "It's a story people are telling to get them through their boring meals. They don't have a life so they make up this man's."

Eddie said, "But not your everyday BS."

"Don't waste your time, Eddie."

Advice from his ex. Listen up, Eddie. Got a notepad? Write this down. Print it so you'll be able to read it later. Eddie said, "So, tell M&M I wanted to talk to her."

"Tell me how Glen is," Patty said.

Eddie, match flame at his Camel, said, "He's seeing UFOs, and he's grabbing his crotch and saying he's half a man." Eddie exhaled smoke, slow, sideways.

Patty said, "Manhood is where the heart is."

"He's impotent," Eddie said.

She said, "For real?"

"For real."

She said, "I can hear him say it. Im-*po*-tunt."

"Perfect," Eddie said.

"Driving Joy crazy, am I right?" Patty said.

Eddie said, "You want to hear the joke about the im-po-tunt

black guy who goes to the doctor? Glen's telling it to anyone who'll stop long enough to listen."

She said, "Let me guess. It ends with the guy saying something like if he's going to be im-po-tunt, he wants to look im-po-tunt."

He said, "You got it."

Patty said, "And the guy has to be black?"

"Wouldn't be the same otherwise."

"Couldn't be British?"

Eddie said, "British can't be black?"

"You know what I mean," she said.

Eddie did. His dad had himself a world view. No doubt about it. Strode about big in the chest. Affirmed in his thinking. Glen belonged in chaps. Eddie said, "No. Not on your life. Has to be black."

Patty said, "How's Joy?" Eddie's mother and Patty were pals. And doers. Go-getters. The kind of people who set things straight. The world's salt and pepper. Neither one messed around. If there was a job to do, they stepped up and, not saying a word, they did it. The two of them together could have, hand in hand, improved the Red Cross.

Eddie said, "Homesick, I think."

"She planting up a storm?"

"As usual." Eddie watched his Camel burn. He knocked ash to the ground. He said, "You doing okay?"

Patty said, "Everything's coming up roses."

He said, "'There's that bright golden haze on the meadow?'"

She said, "'The corn is as high as an elephant's eye'"—sort

of sang the line. Like she was accepting that life wasn't no musical even if you could sing the tunes and hit the high notes.

"That's tall," he said.

This was familiar ground. Show tunes. Their version of footsies.

"I'll tell Maggie your heart is thumping for her," Patty said. "Call tomorrow night, early."

Eddie let his Camel burn down in his fingers. Lit a fresh cigarette. He offered Roscoe one. The toad remained inscrutable.

"Don't be such a toad," Eddie said to Roscoe. Couldn't coax a smile out of him.

Ohio was busy being noisy. Two dogs from up the street barking. One then the other one. There were screeches in the trees. Crickets on microphones. Bullfrogs gone moon-crazy. All of it accented because the cicadas had shut up. Daytime, wherever you walked you crushed bugs. They stuck to your clothes. They landed in your hair. A local checkout lady at Kroger's told Eddie their coming was one more fact to add to the already overwhelming evidence that the year 2000 would bring with it the end of the world. The cicadas swarmed the trees, smothered the air with their song, which built, through the humid mornings, to a thrumming electrical hum you had to yell to be heard over. They had a short time to get their business done, to beat and drum their chests and get the eggs fertilized. The cicada's joyride. Sex. Sex. Sex. Perpetuate themselves. Who could blame them?

Tomorrow, when he called, Eddie hoped to tell M&M what the newspapers were saying about the cicadas, and she would beg for more. She would hang up and rush to her room, to the

Book of Knowledge, C through D. No, more likely she would be on the Internet before Eddie stepped away from the phone. M&M would be the one to tell Eddie there were three varieties. She would explain how he could distinguish the male from the female. She would describe their eyes as Red Hots. She would send drawings. She would send him related vocabulary words. She would remind Eddie to get a computer.

"Underground for seventeen years," M&M would say. "It's party time."

Imagine Eddie and Patty years ago. Early in their marriage. Think happy days. They're living in Las Vegas. Imagine Patty dealing him blackjack, her saying, "Cards ain't entertainment. Cards ain't a pastime. Cards is allegory, is business, not unlike the stock exchange."

Her saying to Eddie, "Snap your ears on and pay attention."

Who was Eddie to say no? He sat up straight. Squared his shoulders. He thought, Incoming.

It was after midnight, and Eddie *was* nothing *but* ears. He wasn't about to jeopardize the moment.

Patty was dealing him fate's hand, one shuffle, one cut, the cards life had in store for him. They were sitting up in bed. The hope alive in Eddie's chest was she would cheat for his sake. To do so was in her. She had the talent, and there was their history, and, at this juncture, less headlong and rash than she had been during their salad days, somewhat more cagey now, and not yet the simmering pissed-off she would be in the years ahead, Patty

One Mile Past Dangerous Curve 51

continued to profess a rooting interest in Eddie. She dealt full-time at the Shoe, downtown, Las Vegas, Nevada. Had gifted hands you would have paid six figures to have on your side. For the fun of it, walking Fremont Street to keep from smoking on her breaks, she did card tricks so scary onlookers stepped away, about-faced, and then hotfooted it for the side streets, only, curiosity working them like poetry, to drift back and gather at a distance, then reapproach, wary as stray dogs, furtive, circumspect, spellbound. Heads cocked. *Chicanery?* The canny has its appeal. Who doesn't want to play with fire a little? Patty, not at this minute Eddie's ex—that endgame was a year and a host of misunderstandings and poor calculations down the road—she laid the queen of spades in front of him on the bedspread. She polished off her vodka and smacked her lips. Zeroed in.

"You burn a card?" he said.

"Forgot," Patty said.

"You got to burn one."

"It's late."

"And you're tired."

"Knock on wood," she said, and she did, rapped the headboard.

"But you can't forget," Eddie said. "Because you don't burn, and that makes it bogus. You don't toy with fate. Fate is the big one. It's the crossroads. Capital *F*, capital *A*, capital *T*, capital *E*."

Patty said, "You done?"

He said, "Burn, then turn."

Patty collected Eddie's queen and her card and reshuffled.

He cut, and she sent the top card to bed. She burned it, tucked it home face-up at the bottom of the deck and dealt. Seven of diamonds for Eddie. It was after one A.M., and Maggie, baby M&M, was asleep in her room. Eddie and Patty had had sex. Greedylike. They had baked mint brownies they topped with rainbow sprinkles and dipped in whipped cream, Patty's civility at flood stage. They caught ESPN sports, baseball coming up on its World Series. Now TV was showing Eddie and Patty late-night disaster footage, proof that the end of the world was not some neighborhood rumor. He sipped Johnnie Walker Black Label Old Scotch Whiskey, liquid so ceremonious and smooth surely it was aged in the netherworld, fussed over by teams of angels and bottled by the devil himself.

Patty's mode was the imperative when it came to cards. Or life itself, for that matter. There'd be no woolgathering, no gazing out the window. No rocking back on the hind legs of your chair. If you didn't put your thinking cap on she did it for you. Listen up, she said. Retract your wheels and get ready. Watch and learn.

Her argument had always been Humpty Dumpty was a momma's boy out to get attention. Was in his heart of hearts a show-off who ought to have been ignored.

Next for Eddie, she dealt the five of clubs, that black-hearted give-you-the-finger suit. He acknowledged it as superstition of ignorant mien, but Eddie, in a game of poker, never drew to a club flush. Not on his life. Not that he was a capital-*G* Gambler, not a capital-*P* Player—cold, calculating, alligator-blooded. No, he tended to let his emotions in. To let his gut influence his

One Mile Past Dangerous Curve   53

game. Eddie tipped his good hands, *oh boy oh boy* written all over his face. He couldn't have sandbagged a three-year-old on a freezing day in January.

But tonight was fate—all caps, F-A-T-E, and blackjack. You swallowed what you were dealt. So far, seven of diamonds, five of clubs. Total, twelve. Ugly luck. Thumbs-down. Pratfall coming. A face card on its way and bust. Game over. Patty said, "You're on the brink." Her up-card, the king of hearts, showed its colors.

"Hit," Eddie said.

Diamond, a five. Total seventeen.

Eddie said, "Hit."

"Ah, Eddie," Patty said. She riffled the deck. "You've won or lost, Eddie. There's a time to hit, and there's a time to stay."

He said, "Hit me."

She did. For Eddie the four of diamonds. Seven, five, five, four. Twenty-one, a winner, the mountain climber's way, foot over foot, handhold after handhold, piton to piton. Card to card to card to card.

"Of course," Patty said. "Saints and sinners and drunks."

"Legit?" he said. "No seconds, and nothing off the bottom?" *Had she fudged for him?* was what he was asking. Lady-fingered a card, perhaps that last one she laid down?

She displayed the deck, tip to top, bottom and sides, thisaway and thataway, the burn in place. Patty, affable and largehearted here in the A.M., showed him she had nothing up her sleeve. Besides—what was Eddie, blind?—she was wearing only boxer shorts and a t-shirt. No ballot-box stuffing. On the up and up she was and, ipso facto, the cards she dealt him were

54 Darrell Spencer

bona fide. Were sterling. He drove cross-country to a winning hand, opted for the scenic route, and arrived at this destination. "Destiny," she said.

Eddie tapped each card where it lay. Seven of diamonds, five of clubs, five of diamonds, then the four. Twenty-one. He said, "What you got in the pocket?"

She said, "I'm stiff," and showed Eddie her hole card, squared a five to her king. She dealt herself a card. Had to. House rules. Busted. The jack of spades. She gathered up Eddie's cards and said, "There it is, Eddie. The hand life's dealt you." He lay back in his reward, and she fanned out the four cards right here over his heart. "You're the champ," she said.

Eddie sat up and tucked his winning hand into his wallet on the nightstand. He said, "Who'd hit on seventeen for real?"

"You risked it all, Eddie," Patty said, and she reached across him and placed the rest of the deck next to his wallet. She said, "We were playing for keeps, and now I deserve a back rub."

So he obliged. Even back then, what now felt like a lifetime ago, Eddie harbored a sound, if bluesy, heart.

Eddie drove Glen to O'Bleness Hospital. Joy didn't have what it took. She had hauled him around enough, but Glen needed the help. He was no longer driving.

"I used to be six-four in my socks," Glen said, and he stepped from a set of scales. He came in at six-two. He said, "The incredible shrinking male." He sucked in his gut and said, "I weigh what I did in high school, give or take five pounds."

One Mile Past Dangerous Curve   55

His blood pressure was up, 210 over 105. He joked with the nurse, said, "It's your fault, my dear. Your loveliness has got me revved. My heart is beating a mile a minute. You can hear it if you put your ear to my chest." He invited her to do so.

She said, "Another time."

"Listen," he said. "It's going pit-a-pat. Pit-a-pat."

"No connection to your blood pressure," she said. "Heart medications?"

"Never touch the stuff," Glen said.

She said, "That a yes or a no?"

He said, "I got a bottle," and he dipped into his pocket and handed it to her.

She cut him a look. The woman had the personality of cardboard was what Eddie was thinking. She said, "You take these like you're supposed to?"

"I'm here for an X-ray," Glen said, "not an inquisition." He tapped where he believed his heart resided, grinned, and said to the nurse, "Pit-a-pat, pit-a-pat." She made a note of his medication, racked his chart and directed them to a waiting room. Ugly carpet everywhere, a swirl of colors that made you dizzy if you weren't already. The chairs belonged in a motel lobby. But the art on the walls—it got Eddie's attention. No barns, no meadows, no flowers. No watercolors. Instead, original prints, Renaissance-looking to Eddie. Robust and plump men and women in gardens. Fleshy. Something soft going on. Italian. Clothing more like drapes than what any sane person would put on. Billowing robes and dresses, but heavy-looking at the same time. All of it so at odds with what was going on here. Radiology. Pathology. Blood work. Here was art with a message about the stubborn everlasting obligations between heaven and earth.

Glen wore slacks and a dress shirt today. First time in Ohio Eddie had seen the man in clothes other than a jumpsuit. Glen insisted on his loafers. No socks. He told Eddie he had thought it through. He could kick the shoes off. Bending to untie them required more than Glen had to give at this point.

"I'm not used to all this rigmarole," Glen said. The hospital, its walls, the long corridor they sat near. Strangers touching him. How quiet it was. Everyone under orders to tread lightly. "We mend ourselves in my family," he said. "You use common sense you don't need a doctor. They give you a pill, and it fixes you one way and hurts you in twenty other directions." He flipped a magazine aside and said, "There's a story about my grandfather taking out his own appendix. He used the lid from a tin can."

"And he sewed himself up," Eddie said. "He got some thread out of grandmother's sewing kit or gut from one of the barn cats he shot himself and went to work stitching."

"I'm not saying it's true," Glen said. He stood and walked a few steps away. Talking. Kept his back to Eddie. "I didn't say I believed it. It's the idea of it is what I'm getting at. It's a way of handling your life I'm illustrating for you. We were renegades. Outlaws. We lived by our own rules because sooner or later that's what it will all come down to." He waved his arms at the hospital in general, as an idea. He said, "This is all going to hell in one of those handbaskets. Someday, we'll be on our own in this country, every town, city and person. The government is going to collapse. Then, when something goes wrong, you are going to have to figure out how to solve it all by yourself. It's how we lived in Wyoming. We didn't rely on anyone."

Eddie locked himself up. Wasn't feeding into it. Would have rolled his eyes like some dipshit teenager but the old guy wasn't looking.

"We rode horses," Glen said. He put his hands on his hips. He said, "These are the thin hips of the horseman."

News to Eddie. He said, "You rode?"

"I could have."

"You know how?"

Glen said, "Like riding a bicycle."

"You know what they say," Eddie said.

His father turned on him. Said, "No, I don't know what they say." He was set up either to throw a punch or absorb one. "Is my boy going to tell me? Is Eddie Dancer so full of himself he's going to offer his father a bit of wisdom?"

Eddie got to his feet and said, "I'm holding up my end of the conversation is all."

"Not really," Glen said. "You're not really."

Eddie waited by radiology for about ten minutes. He caught himself trying to count the number of twirls one of the blades in a ceiling fan was making, so he went out front and walked around to the backside of the hospital. He was facing the Hocking River, its water so low and thready in its bed he couldn't see it from here. There had been no rain for a couple of weeks now. From the highway, if you were looking at the river, you saw that islands of high weeds and mud created jigsaw puzzles near the shore.

Canada geese had gathered on the far bank. Across 682, on the hilltop above the road, stood the Ridges, the old asylum, built in the 1870s. It brought prosperity with it—hundreds of government jobs, hundreds of government paychecks, and people to spend that money. The Athens Lunatic Asylum. Ohio politicians fought over where it would be built. Athens won. Contracts were signed and the Masons marched down Court Street. Crowds gathered. Dignitaries spoke. There was American-flag bunting. Eddie could see only corners and roofs of the buildings from where he stood. The trees swallowed them. Over thirteen hundred patients at one time. Close to two hundred on staff. There was one central building, flanked by wings on both sides, all of it four or five stories high. Cottages sat on nearby knolls. The whole shebang was out of business now, had been purchased by the university, and part of the old administration building had been refurbished into an art gallery.

There was a white haze in the air, not fog, not mist, but enough of whatever it was to knock the color out of the sky. A blue heron rose from the bed of the Hocking and flew toward Eddie, then turned downriver.

"Sue them," Glen said. "Call Noah and get the lawyers on the phone. Call Penrod. I'm taking this place for every penny it's got."

A nurse had asked Glen to drink a malt he couldn't keep down. He tried three times. Never did hold it in. The technicians went ahead and took the X-rays, guessing they would turn out.

"We guess?" Glen said. "Some bearded foreign fucker said, 'We guess.' What is this, a crapshoot?"

Eddie helped him move along.

"Fly-by-night," he said to Eddie. "Flimflam. I'm betting you can buy snake oil here."

They had gotten to the lobby, and Glen was loud. Not deaf loud. Crowd loud. "Bastards," he said, Eddie at his side, steadying him. They walked a few feet. Stopped. Glen was stuck in the doorway. He was pale, and his hands shook. His hair was a mess, was smashed to his scalp like he had been egged.

"You want to sit?" Eddie said.

"No. Hell no. Shit no," Glen said. "Get me out of here."

In the truck, Eddie reached across and buckled Glen in. Glen closed his eyes and said, "I appreciate it. You're a good boy."

Sure, Eddie thought. Give the boy a stick.

"Do you think that was enough?" Glen said.

Eddie said, "Of the drink?"

"No. Of the X-ray," Glen said. "Do you think that was enough of the X-ray?"

Eddie said, "They know how to do their job."

"Do you think it killed the cancer?"

Eddie pulled onto West Union before he answered. He said, "Dad, it wasn't for that."

"I'm not stupid," Glen said. "I understand what *X-ray* means. I didn't say it was for that." He shut his eyes and said, "But it's radiation, all the same. No harm in wondering."

Days later, when the doctor phoned—Joy took the call—the news was that the cancer had spread. More hot spots on Glen's ribs. Glen's bags were packed. The doctors reciting the old story: six months. Maybe a year.

Joy said to Eddie, "So what your father says to me is, 'They took my balls for nothing.'" She told Glen the surgery had slowed it down, and he said, "Waste of time. Waste of everybody's time." He wouldn't look at Joy. He said, "The quicker the better. Let's get on with it. The quicker the better."

One a.m., dewy Ohio, Eddie on his cordless, outside the trailer, sitting on top of the redwood table. A dad talking to his daughter, Roscoe the toad riding shotgun at Eddie's side, Roscoe bulky like he had put on weight. Glen, above, on the balcony to his and Joy's bedroom, drifted in and out of the house, taking photos, flashes of light popping. He was documenting the cicada fling. Had been for a couple of weeks. The bugs shut up at night, but were crawling everywhere, on patios, windows, planter pots, cars. Glen taped his photographs to a wall in the kitchen. He was putting together a collage. He overlapped pictures, so they seemed to stutter, snapshots of cicadas swarming the decks, bushes, trees, shrubs. One photo of a cicada doing a handstand on a clothesline. He photographed the funnel-shaped mounds they crawled out of. He caught two mating and off-set a series of prints on top of each other. One sequence of pictures above the breakfast counter captured a cicada husking its shell.

Every morning, a local woman on talk radio was interviewing cicadas. It had become a popular bit. People were tuning in.

One Mile Past Dangerous Curve   61

She was talking to bugs on the air. She would step outside the studio, and one would land on her microphone. She would say, "You're looking sharp this morning."

You would hear the cicada buzz like short-circuit. It varied, from crisp to gruff, one brassy, another chirring, one shrill. Alto, soprano, falsetto. The bugs could be raspy and screechy. Stentorian. Cranky. As if this were a real conversation the lady and the cicada were having. She asked the cicadas in because they were the experts on living the sudden but intense life.

"You liking Athens?" the talk-show lady would say.

The cicada response sounded like a party favor. Like a tin clicker. They had range and could riff.

The lady would say, "Did we pupate today?"

Eddie, phone at his ear, had talked Patty into waking Maggie, and he was telling his daughter about Liar's Corner Road and his drive to Cotton's. "More trees growing in one square mile than you can find in the whole state of Nevada," he said. He gave a Camel to his lips.

"You're being hyperbolic," she said.

Fifteen years old? His daughter? Her vocabulary.

Above Eddie, on the balcony, another flash. He hopped off the table and moved toward the house. He winked at Roscoe. The toad sat mum, heavy as a doorstop. "Cross my heart," Eddie said to M&M. "They call it Liar's Corner Road. I turn on it and up a hill I go. Only first gear will hold me—it's so steep, and the front end's about to flip back and over. My tires are spitting gravel. Traction is slippery. I'm hanging onto the steering wheel with both hands. I should be wearing those gloves race-car drivers use. There are ruts on both sides you can play hide-and-seek in, and it's high noon here in the heartland."

M&M said, "There's danger on both sides."

He said, "There's danger all around."

She said, "As far as the eye can't see."

There you go, he thought. His daughter turning the world upside down and looking at it in fresh ways. "You got the picture," he said. "Woods so thick you'd have to turn sideways and move real slow to get anywhere in them. You couldn't run. You'd kill yourself, have a head-on with a tree trunk. There'd be no way to have a picnic. No place to sit. Nowhere to spread a tablecloth." He walked toward the house, managed to get a match to his cigarette. Lit it. Coughed. He said, "You could be one foot from someone and not see them."

Maggie said, "From the serial killer."

"He could tap you on the shoulder," Eddie said, "and there's no way you'd see it coming."

She said, "You'd have to be way skinny."

"Way more than you can imagine." Eddie exhaled and said, "At the top I think the truck is about to fall off the side. There's road, which is as wide as a popsicle stick. There's no leeway, no forgiveness, no room for error. It's ditch is all. Old Toyota is airborne, or so it seems—hood in my face—and on the other side, headed down, it's so dark I turn the lights on. No sun getting through, and I can't see my hand in front of my face."

Maggie said, "You're exaggerating for effect."

"Truth be told, I'm swearing on all I hold sacred," he said, and he used his cigarette hand to cross his heart.

M&M said, "Truth be told?"

One Mile Past Dangerous Curve   63

He said, "Heartland talk."

"Do they say, 'Neighbor, how you doing?'"

"That's Texas."

"What do you hold sacred, Eddie?" M&M said.

No question for a fifteen-year-old to be asking her father long-distance and in the middle of the night. "Plenty," he said. He tried to think of one thing and couldn't. Not right this minute.

Maggie said, "Your story, the drive, Liar's Corner—you're pulling my leg all the way off and putting it on backwards." She had let her dad off the hook.

Precocity. You could be too smart at M&M's age. You could peak too soon. Shirley Temple was your red flag. All that glory, and then where were you for the next sixty years?

Eddie described Charles Cotton and his ranch house in the middle of what seemed to be nowhere unless you had your panoramic, bird's-eye view from a helicopter, unless you could see from above that ten minutes in any direction through the thick trees and you would be on a decent road. Eddie talked until Maggie said, "You are coming back to Las Vegas? I mean, you're not gone, right?"

Eddie wasn't gone. He owned his bungalow in Boulder City out near Lake Mead. He had a life. He said to Maggie, "Your father here, he's got a big-time love for you."

She said, "Yeah, me too."

He said, "Returning—that's the plan, Stan." He had reached the steps of the house. Above, yet another flash.

Maggie said, "Get on the train, Wayne."

"M&M," he said, "I'll see you sooner than you think," and

64 Darrell Spencer

she said, "A girl needs her dad," so that after a couple of shut-down minutes, he hung up, telling Maggie to tell Patty *muchas gracias* for fetching her, for letting him and his daughter have this quality time, and Maggie saying, "I'm counting the days, partner."

So was Eddie.

And then he said it. Right now, a foot here in the heartland, he said to his smart and savvy daughter, to his child, "You, M &M. I hold you sacred."

"Yeah," she said.

He said, "Yeah," the way you can, the way that word can mean everything there is to say.

M&M said, "Eddie, does anything matter?"

"You," he said. "You matter."

Blame Eddie's being in Ohio on his DNA. Put him on a couch and see if upbringing was at the root of his coming. Guilt? Love? Fate's hand—the one Patty dealt him? He'd gotten that phone call from Joy, and he was here in three days.

The vectors of fate and character colliding.

Joy was saying Glen was acting scary. The Lone Ranger in Eddie rose up, and he had driven through the night.

Eddie opened the slider and stepped into the living room. He felt like a burglar. Light-footed. Not an unpleasant posture. He called out Glen's name. Then Joy's. A TV was on upstairs, loud enough to lengthen cracks in the walls.

Eddie heard Glen yelling. That voice the man used. Pontificating. Probably, to Glen's way of thinking, God's tone. Glen did have his God. The Lord God Mr. Fix It. You do this, and you do that, and things will fall out as they ought. Glen employed his oracle voice from his getting up in the morning to his going to bed at night. He had to be heard. Your assignment was to pay attention. Undivided. No grab-assing while Glen talked. You sat in the front row. You didn't rock on your feet. Glen kept his end of the teeter-totter pinned to the ground, and you, on your side, were suspended in the air, legs dangling. He was, as an adult, the playground bully.

Only the lamp next to Joy was on. The TV lit the room. Then faded some. No sound coming from it. Joy sat on her half of the bed, legs over the side, her pink comforter bunched at her hip.

Glen's closet was open, and there was a box full of videos on the floor. On the bed, more. *Sexual Positions for Lovers. Erotic Women. Big-Busted Platinum. Flesh Gordon.*

"You're just in time to settle a dispute," Glen said to Eddie. He spoke from the balcony. He aimed his camera toward the house and said, "Say cheese." The flash burst. There was something goat-like in the man's shoulders. Narrow. Stingy. He stepped inside, came through the upstairs slider and said, "You can help us through a disagreement of the fundamental kind." He sat and hunched forward on a chair he pulled in close to Joy. Put them toe to toe. He crowded her. He was in his underwear and a t-shirt.

"What are you doing?" Eddie said.

Glen showed Eddie his camera. "I'm taking photographs," Glen said. "Of the bugs at night. They're undressing out there. They're walking out of their bodies and coming alive."

Joy said, "There's no disagreement here." What she was

saying—and Eddie heard this loud and clear—was, *Where Glen is, there is Glen's way. End of discussion.*

"I'm telling your mother about Noah's boys," Glen said.

Joy tucked her legs up, onto the bed, under the covers. Glen had served her a cup of worms. He had not been talking about Noah's boys. Eddie, at the top of the stairs, had overheard him say *Bullshit.* Then, *And you know it.* Followed by, *That's a lie.* Glen was yelling at Joy. He said, *You know it. I know it.* He said, *Who keeps track of where you go all day. When you'll be back. Who you see?*

It turned out that Noah's boys, the twins, had asked their father into his den and told him they no longer believed in God. His gifted boys, his twins who, at nine, had invented a card game they called Double Trouble. Noah never quite caught on when he played with them. The game mixed pinochle and draw poker.

"Might as well not believe in gravity for all the good it will do you to deny his existence," Glen said.

Joy said, "They're teenagers—"

"They're snotnosed little shits."

Joy bowed her head.

"Pissants," Glen said. "You see their hair? Dyed. The color of a girl's. Like flowers. They're queer ducks and skinny in that sissy way. They say to their father, to Noah, 'Sit down, Noah.' *Noah?* These are children. Kids. I don't care if their IQs are bigger than Einstein's. This is in their father's den, where he does his business and makes the money they spend. They call their father Noah. They say, 'Noah, have a seat.'"

Eddie's spin on what he learned from Glen was that Noah's

boys took on the adults in an adult way. Nothing against their father and nothing against his God. "We're agnostic," one of them said to Noah. The other one said they had listened to their hearts on this one.

So, according to Glen, in Noah's den it was Noah and his boys, Matthew and Mark. Imagine, then, the small fry swimming against the current. Asking their father into his den. You can see the drama. Noah, a little pudgy. He had to twist his clothes to get into them that morning. He ushered his boys in, not sure what it was they wanted. But proud. Olive Root, in the hallway, caught his eye. He shrugged. She shrugged. Neither could guess what was going on. The boys so adult, so grown-up. Noah's honor-roll boys. The twins, who, one summer, taught themselves sign language because they liked how it felt to move their fingers and hands that way. Full academic scholarships, and Matthew would be on the swim team. Mark, soccer. Mark planned to study law, corporate, maybe become a sports agent. Matthew was thinking medicine. Research, though—no patients. No time for them. Noah hesitated before he shut the door, buffed each shoe against a pant leg.

What Noah stepped into was a lounge act, the twins doing bad-cop bad-cop. "Monkeyshines," Glen said to Eddie and Joy in the dark bedroom. Matthew and Mark got in their dad's face, and they spelled it out for him, started with the which-came-first-the-chicken-or-the-egg questions. Effect or cause? Cart before the horse. The logistics of situation and circumstance. Socks before shoes, right? Maybe not. One could posit a situation that called for shoes before socks. Think on it. You could imagine such a need. Nothing was cut and dried. Noah was not dumb. They granted him his business acumen. They praised his work ethic. Matthew and Mark crossed their legs at the knee. They had been to the oracle and in its presence refused to limit themselves to yes-or-no questions.

You can hear them.

You can hear Noah wondering what all this had to do with his boys and God.

"Reason," Matthew said to his father. "Where does it get you?" He huffed.

Mark said, "Thinking hard, what good is it in the end?"

"Pounding the pavement of the mind."

"Plumbing the depths."

"Fielding the tough questions."

"The mind always tearing its own house down."

Matthew and Mark, these seventeen-year-olds, they had honed their act. It was as if they had prepared for this moment since they were five years old. All that pantomime they had done over the years. Now they were opening with a concession. They admitted the folly of human thought, particularly thought about thought. Matthew said, "A quantum theory of gravity. Fat chance. Wishful thinking. Disneyland for smart people. Like Las Vegas, the badlands turned theme park."

All the time Noah thinking, You're kids. What do you know? Really know?

The material of human life was transported to earth by asteroids? Give Mark a break. Run him over with a fire engine. Might as well.

"Fodder," Matthew said.

Noah hid his eyes. He later told Glen he turned to God at this point. Leaked a silent prayer. "Touch their hard hearts," he whispered to God. "They're young." Next morning he was up at four A.M., on his knees again, saying, "They know not what they do."

But in his den he uncovered his eyes and there was the devil in his boys' faces. He saw in their eyes the red you see in bad snapshots. Their smiles were sneers.

Imagine that.

And more.

Noah squirmed in his chair, and his boys laid bare the roots of the cosmic arts. Matthew, elbows on his father's fat desk, lisped. He said, "What's your sign, Dad?"

Reason, it was nothing to shout about.

Matthew turned on a desk lamp, and Mark fingered shadows on the wall, numbers. 6 6 6. "Frightening," the boys said.

"Quicksand," Mark said.

Matthew said, "No hero to the rescue."

Noah's soul got down on its knees and thumped out a second message to God. *They're terribly young*, it said. The soul's Morse code. *SOS*, it said. *Mayday. Mayday.*

Their concession complete, Matthew and Mark turned the spotlight on religion. They told Noah they had taken their doubts to the Egyptian Scales of Maut, where Matthew placed on the left tray the symbol of their frazzled minds, a plastic dashboard Jesus, and Mark floated a white feather of justice on the right tray. They waited. Three hours. Three days. Three months. Their burden got no lighter. Nothing washed.

So at seventeen, they spoke three languages, read another two, did fringe mathematics for R & R, and now they had come to kick over the traces.

"We're agnostic," they said.

They said, "We're not atheists."

"Where did we come from?" Noah said. "Who created us?"

"From stones licked by cows." The twins spoke in stereo. In a wicked unison accompanied by a soft-shoe afoot in their throats. They said, "It's all once upon a time. We created us in our own image."

Noah said, "Why are we alive on this earth?"

"To slay dragons." A duet.

"What happens after we die?"

"You know that one," they said. "Dust," Matthew said, pointing at Mark, and Mark, pointing at Matthew, said, "to dust."

It occurred to Noah that he had forgotten that all was God's will. He overreached, had asked for more than it was his place to ask for. He had coveted women, other men's wives. He left the boys' mother, a dutiful lady, and married a secretary, a stranger, really. For sex. He admitted it. He begged God's forgiveness. Then he divorced her, and now here was Olive Root. Maybe some heartfelt humbler-than-thouing was in order. Was called for. To God, Noah said, "If it is to be, it is to be, as is thy will in all things. Thy will be done. Not my will. All according to thy will." He thought, This shouldn't happen to a dog on a hot day in August.

Joy located the remote on the bed and shut the TV off. Glen said to her, "They're a disappointment to their father." He turned toward Eddie and said, "There is the gloom of hell, and the glory of heaven, and Noah's boys will get their rewards. They'll eat their words."

One Mile Past Dangerous Curve   71

Glen's theory was you did things because they were right. You didn't do other things. They were wrong. The difference was clear-cut. Commandments and laws and interdictions—they held the world together. Glen believed life was a case of black and white. He told you that and he flipped his hand palm up and said, "Black." He turned his hand over, said, "White." Living was like tuning a car. You could do it half-assed and fly-by-night, and the car plugged along, or you could do it according to the book. God, as Eddie knew, as Joy knew, as Noah knew, as all those around Glen knew, was someone you talked to. Face to face. The Bible said *face to face*. Ergo, a mouth, a nose, eyes. Would God be a real person if he didn't have a face? Would he appear in a burning bush if he didn't have our best interests in mind? Allow himself to be nailed to a cross and spit on? Die for us?

"Glen," Joy said, "they're smart kids doing what smart kids do."

Glen said, "Smart. What is smart? Grades in school." The man was on fire. He all but spit. "Yale," he said. "There's a hell-hole if there ever was one." He was unglued. He said, "Smart." More a shriek than a word.

Joy tossed her covers aside.

"What kind of smart is not having a God?" Glen said.

Eddie said, "Who believes in God still?"

"Who believes in God?" Glen said.

"It's the end of the twentieth century," Eddie said. "Who even talks about God unless you're running for office or if the newspapers catch you being bad in public and print your picture?"

Glen said, "Who believes in God?"

72 Darrell Spencer

"Who cares? That's what I'm saying," Eddie said. "God's not even a subject anymore."

Joy was on her way off the bed. Glen stood. He climbed over himself to get himself on his feet, and she hesitated and sat back. He said to Eddie, "You—" Caught himself. He wasn't breathing well. He coughed and staggered. He said, "It's all signs of the last days. Men in earrings. Tattoos."

There was a photograph Eddie knew Joy kept of her and Glen ballroom dancing at the Flamingo in Las Vegas. Colorized. His father is reaching for his mother, Glen in white tails, his hair so dark and short it looks like he has yanked on a swimmer's cap. He is wearing white gloves. The tails to his jacket are stiff. Joy's in a lime-green dress, chiffon. She wears gloves to her elbows. The song they danced to—one of them, Joy once told Eddie—was Nat King Cole's "Almost Like Being in Love."

The only light in the room came from the one lamp. Joy hauled herself to the other side of the bed. She said, "Your father saw a flying saucer on his walk."

"Shit," Glen said.

Joy said, "He told me he did."

"I'm seeing what I'm seeing," Glen said.

Eddie wanted out. Was feeling like he was hog-tied and duct-taped to a chair.

Glen said, "The government's hiding the evidence."

"You're watching too much TV," Eddie said. "You're wearing the subject out. Talk about stupid."

"You can explain the crop circles?" Glen said. "Those cattle all over the West, dead, but not gone? Mutilated is all. Their lips removed, their eyelids cut away by something as precise as a laser only more so, and the carcass drained of blood, but there is no blood anywhere on the ground. You figured out how it's done, have you, genius?"

"Who thinks about it?" Eddie said.

Glen said, "Like God. Right, Ace?"

"Sure, like God. Who goes around thinking about God? Who cares?" Eddie said. "Spaceships. God. It's all the same. It has nothing to do with life. Who really cares?"

Glen said, "Anyone who gives a fuck, that's who."

Eddie reached the bedroom door, heard Glen say, "Your mother wants to put me in a home where I can join hands with other old coots and tap dance."

First Eddie had heard of this. Joy's face told him Glen was lying. The old guy was making it up. Prevaricating for the hell of it. Out of a sense of duty to his condition.

"You sit in wheelchairs," Glen said. "Blankets on your knees. Us old guys, the dying, we can't even get Saint Peter up, much less shake it all about. It sits in my pants as useless as my bum ear. It's a decoy. I could unzip and no one would complain. Feel threatened? By what, dead meat? Hell, us old guys, we manage to get our pants on and they give us a standing ovation." He grabbed his crotch. He said, "Your mother here, she wants to retire me someplace where the inmates play catch with sponges. She wants to be free to bring her men here to the house."

Joy was on her feet, and she squeezed past Glen, who had two-stepped over to block her way.

"Fuck it," Glen said.

74 Darrell Spencer

Joy was crying. She said to Eddie, "I never—"

"Not even a yellow dog will wag its tail," Glen said. He started after Joy and Eddie cut him off.

Eddie said, "You really are a piece of work."

"Good for you, boy," Glen said. "Stick up for your mom. Never say die. Keep your mother's spirits going. Who would have thought it? She'll need your help."

Eddie turned to follow Joy down the hall.

Glen said, "Bravo. Hear. Hear."

Eddie faced him. Was this the time for the son to throw that overhand right, the haymaker, the one that all boys needed to let loose?

"Bully for you," Glen said. He pumped a fist for his boy and said, "Let's cheer for standing up and being counted." He took a boxer's stance and said, "Show me something. Fight, boy. Fight."

"You're a sad case," Eddie said.

Glen said, "I know my way around the streets. I never brought the world's crap home with me, but I'm no dope." He sat on the bed, dropped to it, like he had taken a spill. He said, "Your father's advice for you is *fuck it*."

Eddie headed for the stairs, and Glen was off the bed, following, trailing after him, talking at Eddie. "Godspeed," Glen said. "Godspeed."

Eddie stopped and turned around. He was a few steps down the stairs and was looking up at the old coot, Glen's head cocked the way he had described it earlier, the way he had held it for the crazy lady in the neighborhood. Eddie said, "You having fun, are you?"

One Mile Past Dangerous Curve   75

Drought? No one was saying so. Not yet. You weren't even to whisper the word. A month and no rain. No big deal.

The crew who mowed Joy's lawn stopped in twice to say they would be by the next week. No use cutting grass that wasn't growing. She rolled out the hoses and spot-watered brown areas. Crabgrass was taking over.

Drought?

Not yet. But coming.

It turned out the lady at Cotton's was A.J. She was his daughter. She met Eddie at the gate off Liar's Corner and trailed him up the road, her hand on the side of the Toyota's bed. She had chopped hair. Cut sharp, oragamied, bossy. Bobby-pinned. It was gumption hair. She was in biker boots, Levi's and a black silk shirt, fringe swinging across its yoke, front and back, beadwork and silver stars on the sleeves. The shirt was half country western, half Hell's Angel. Eddie was delivering one of Cotton's signs—MIRACLES COME IN CANS NOT IN CAN'TS. He had planned on snapping a couple of lines and using single-stroke letters, but got caught up in what he was doing and the result was a sign he could have sold on Broadway. Mint-green background against a lemon yellow and a poppy red. Cotton wanted the M in MIRACLES to be fancy, ornate, and Eddie went him twenty better, created an M for the ages, used sixteen colors— highlights in royal purple, crimson, Russian blue, hooker green, Cademon orange—and gold leafing. It was larger than the other letters and hinged, off-set slightly into the border. Atkinson Fancy Roman lettering. Woven into the M were vines and flowers. Background was shrubbery and trees and their roots, and if you studied the foliage, you could locate a baby asleep in a crib, lambs suckling nearby.

Eddie, A.J., and Cotton, Rolling Rock in their hands, sat on the edge of the porch and celebrated the sign. "Lordy, lordy, lordy," Cotton said. The three of them touched beers, and Cotton said, "Eddie, I'm stealing from you. You're spending a fortune."

Eddie admitted the cost.

"We'll settle up," Cotton said. "In the end you'll come out fine on this." He gave Eddie a bundle of messages written on three-by-five cards. One said simply COUNT YOUR BLESSINGS. Another one was EXERCISE DAILY / WALK WITH GOD.

Eddie stuck them in his pocket and said, "You'll excuse me, I hope. I got to see a man at Big Bear." The grocery store had hired him to do a week's worth of butcher-paper spring-madness signs. *Idaho Potatoes 37 Cents a Pound. Cantaloupe 3 for $1. Brawny Paper Towels / Buy One Multi-Pack Get One Free.*

"You want to give me a lift?" A.J. said.

Eddie looked to Cotton, who was gathering up their empties. Eddie said, "If I can."

"I'm headed where you're headed," A.J. said. She needed to pick up her car. Had had the oil changed and the tires rotated.

Sure, company was fine with Eddie. She went into the house for her purse, and Cotton walked Eddie over to the Toyota. Eddie fired it up. He lit a Camel. Cotton said, "Still got your Nevada plates on."

One Mile Past Dangerous Curve   77

"I'm not staying," Eddie said. "This adventure is temporary."

Cotton said, "Not happy here?"

"I need sky," Eddie said.

"Your daughter?" Cotton said. "You miss her?"

Like the dickens. Eddie said, "Her, too. Her more than sky."

"It sounds like she's a good one."

"She's a bright light in the universe."

No. A.J. didn't know what Cotton was doing with the signs. No. He wasn't a nut case. No. She hadn't lived here long. Had been back only a year. *Back?* Eddie wondered. Five years ago, she spent two months in Ohio with Cotton when he returned. *Returned?* Cotton grew up in Athens. He left when he was eighteen and ended up in New York City. Now he was home. Eddie wondered why A.J. moved back. To be with Pop, she told him, and because of a job. She was substitute-teaching history and civics at Federal Hocking High School in The Plains, this with her Ph.D. from Berkeley.

"In fact," she told Eddie, "I taught your brother's boys when they came in."

"Noah's a stepbrother —or half?" Eddie said. "Same father, different mothers, so whatever that makes us."

A.J. said, "His kids are smart cookies."

"Gifted," Eddie said. "Their mother made sure you understood that the official word was gifted."

They had taken 33 into town, hit the off-ramp and were waiting for the light on East State. City workers, two women, were replanting flowers in the median.

"You're right. You pick it up in class in about two seconds," A.J. said. "Those two boys energize the air around them. It's like they could combust. They also excel at clowning around."

"Noah tells me so," Eddie said.

"They're also—" A.J. hesitated. Eddie glanced at her, giving her the okay, the go-ahead. Speak your mind, he was saying. She said, "They're running with skinheads. Kids the other kids say are Klan boys."

"Mark and Matthew?"

"They're the ones."

"Actual skinheads? The real thing?"

"That's what I heard."

"That's crazy."

"It can be more than crazy."

"They're going to Yale next year."

"Sure, they're smart enough."

A.J. went to Big Bear with Eddie and shopped while he took care of business. Back at the dealer, her car wasn't ready. A recall the computer caught at the last minute needed to be resolved, something to do with the seal on the oil pan. "Kill an hour with me?" Eddie said. "I'm meeting Noah in Nelsonville."

"Ah," she said, "Victorian Nelsonville."

They retook 33 out of town. No clouds, but a thin whiteness lay against the sky. Until a little over a year ago A.J., her Ph.D. framed and stashed in a drawer, was operations officer for Bank of America in Anaheim, California. The job nearly killed her. There were personality issues in every drawer. Everybody who worked there was half-cocked and slaphappy and ready to pick a fight. It was all the time cloak-and-dagger, so she quit.

Eddie slowed for a light south of Nelsonville, and A.J. said, "You want to know if he killed his wife?"

"If he did, I don't," Eddie said.

"She's alive and kicking up her heels in San Francisco," A.J. said. They passed the Dairy Queen, could see the Snapper shop going up. Noah was one month behind schedule. A.J. said, "But he was married before, so it's possible he murdered the other one. That wife would be too old to be my mother."

"Your mother's in San Francisco?"

"I talked to her last night."

"So he's been married twice," Eddie said.

She said, "Five times all together."

"Really bad luck or dumb choices?"

"He claims his love is always deep if not long."

Eddie said, "If there were five, it sounds like the mystery is still alive and well. He could have killed one of them somewhere along the way."

Eddie's business with Noah was signs he was painting for the opening of the Snapper franchise. Eddie parked out front. Noah was talking to a man in an orange hard hat. Olive Root walked across a bridge of planks toward Eddie and A.J., and Eddie said to A.J., "Here comes your treat, the woman heading our way. Hang in there. She might be playing with a full deck, but it's not the deck everyone else is using."

He introduced A.J., and Olive Root said to her, "You're new." On meeting Olive Root, you assumed she was host to some kind of strange and colorful bird. Today, she looked like she had climbed out of bed and put her mouth on upside down. Her pioneer-woman's skirt wrapped around her like bunting.

She bought and wore only men's shoes. Never wore a bra. Liked tie-dye and paisley. Something about her hair was like a rosebush in winter. It was reddish brown and brittle, a thicket. It looked as if she combed it with a pitchfork. She said to A.J., "I saw you at the high school. I was there to see about the boys. About some misbehaving they'd done. They get bored—are too hyper for the day-to-day stuff schools do—and they like to shake things up."

"Did we meet?" A.J. said.

"No one introduced us, if that's what you mean," Olive Root said. "I saw you was all, and I have terrific visual recall, like a photographic memory for what I see."

A.J. said, "You never forget a face."

Olive Root said, "Not on your life."

Noah wandered over, his clownish walk on display, as if there were jingling bells on the toes of his shoes. He had skid-mark hair, thin and stringy on top where it screeched straight backwards. He kept his black beard trimmed tight as Velcro. Noah was six-two. Rocky-eyed and always tiptoeing along the edge of some cliff. He said, "Nothing comes easy."

Eddie said, "You got troubles?"

"Troubles. God, no. Not this. Not building on clay. Not dealing with a bunch of tree lovers who think doing business is against Mother Nature's will," Noah said. "They don't want a Wal-Mart. They don't want a mall. 'Got one,' they're saying. *What about the local businesses? What about the local businesses?* Damn broken record. They're fighting progress every inch of the way." Noah patted himself down, hunting a cigarette. He had none. Had quit. He said, "There is no local economy. You can't buy a decent shirt within a hundred miles of this burg. I tried."

Eddie said, "You still want the signs?"

"Only one," Noah said. He reached for A.J.'s hand and said, "I've seen you."

"I teach your boys," she said.

"Jesus," Noah said. He touched Eddie's arm and said, "Week ago they pack and drive away. Day after they turned eighteen. We have a party, and nothing's wrong. We're all laughing and talking, and Olive Root baked a cake big as a tire, which we polished off. Next morning, Mark puts his arm around my shoulders, and he says, 'We'll keep in touch.' Matthew gives me this smart-alecky wink was all."

Eddie said, "Where to? Where did they go?"

Noah said, "No idea."

Olive Root said, "They're of an age."

Noah said, "Angie calls every ten minutes. She's paid for Fordham. Where are Mark and Matthew? She had a deal with them. Fordham costs a fortune. What kind of shit am I trying to pull."

"She's driving me up a wall," Olive Root said.

Noah said, "I told her to come on out if she thought she could find them."

Eddie asked if Noah knew if the boys had stayed in Ohio.

"They could be in Florida for all they told me," Noah said. "Or Los Angeles."

"If I was a betting woman," Olive Root said, "I'd say they're within shouting distance."

Eddie said, "A.J. tells me they're running with skinheads."

"You saw them?" Noah said to her.

"One of the teachers mentioned it, is all," A.J. said.

Noah said, "Shit. Nazis. Is that what you're saying?"

A.J. said, "Maybe it's just people telling stories, how they do."

Noah shook his head. He led Eddie around the side of the building, talking about how the city was limiting him to the one sign. He wanted to show Eddie where it would go. Olive Root attached herself to A.J., and they followed Eddie and Noah, close enough that Eddie could hear Olive Root. "I've got ideas," she was saying. Eddie sneaked a look at the two of them, heard Olive Root say, "Did you see *Easy Rider?* Peter Fonda. Dennis Hopper. You know, that movie that made Jack Nicholson who he is today. I saw it probably one hundred times. I went back and back. How could you not? What can you say about a film like that? Peter Fonda, he should be president of our country. Of the United States. You know? I mean you see him now and it's right in front of your eyes that he's taken on the mantle of his generation. Of mine. You know? He's a wise you can be only when you've walked down a hard road. When you've stumbled and gotten yourself up. You have to go whole hog all the way down into hell in order to come out the other side." Olive Root walked and she sang bits and pieces of Beatles songs. *I am the egg man. Penny Lane is in your eyes and in your ears.* She said to A.J., "You read *Rolling Stone* magazine?"

A.J. told her she had noticed it around.

They caught up to Eddie and Noah. "Did you see *The Graduate?*" Olive Root said to all of them. "You can't be the same after you sat through it. It's the movie that rescued Dustin

Hoffman from oblivion." She hunkered down her face so she was the spitting image of Dustin Hoffman, and, trying for that dry delivery, that brain-dead affect Hoffman pulled off, she said, "'No, sir. It's completely baked.'" Olive Root stepped around and took Noah's arm. She said, "After Dylan, after *The times they are a changin'*. After Woodstock. You feel it. The spirit. Rock changed the world. It stopped Vietnam. Whatever kind of music ever did that before? They're doing another Woodstock like that other one they tried. Joe Cocker rasping out his limp-dick music for corporate America. MTV is shit, you know."

"Sex," A.J. said. "Sex, I think, changed the world, if we go back to the beginning."

Olive Root tugged at her hair. She said, "Rock changed sex."

A.J. said, "I meant the world. Sex changed the world. Rock came along for the ride."

Olive Root seemed to recede. She was stumped. She let go of Noah and wrung her hands. Some nut had taped a row of dynamite to Olive Root's waist and had a thumb on the detonator. She gathered together clumps of her hair and hauled the bundle from one side to the other as if she had gotten hold of a ferret she had attached to herself.

"It's a joke," A.J. said. "It's an old joke. You see, you say that rock changed sex, and—"

Some bad chord struck here. Olive Root twitchy.

A.J. said, "You know, Adam? Eve? The snake?"

Olive Root was gone. She was backing up. Was not dealing with this, whatever it was. She went into the building.

84   Darrell Spencer

Eddie, A.J., and Noah circled back to Eddie's truck, and Eddie and A.J. got in. Eddie told Noah he had hired Huntington Bark to build the sign. Noah leaned into the truck and said, "Eddie, you see what Glen's doing to Joy." He glanced at A.J.

"I do," Eddie said.

Noah said, "We need to help."

"If we can," Eddie said, and Noah stepped away from the window.

"It's not good," he said.

Eddie said, "It's worse than not good."

"Family shit," Eddie said, and A.J. nodded. They had returned to the car dealership. He spent the drive telling her about Glen and Joy, about Pastor Davis, the gun.

She said, "Family shit."

One of the universals.

Glen said, "You know the one about the two old ladies in the mall?" He had Eddie trapped out back of the house, and Eddie was feeling pinned down. Under fire. He was working on one of Cotton's signs.

"You're talking about the ladies with the painted-desert hair?" Eddie said.

"That's the one."

"The ladies with skin the color of light bulbs?"

"You got it. The look of onions. They're talking," Glen said. "Two of them. If you saw the pair of them you'd say they're having a grand time. They're going on and on about the good old days like they haven't seen each other for twenty years. They brag about their children. One's got twelve grand-kids, and the other one has fifteen. They've got great-grand-kids. So many they get them confused. They'll show you the pictures if you want to see them. Even the men their daughters married are handsome and kind to these old crones. One of their grandkids, a girl, is going to end up president of the United States."

Eddie said, "I can see them."

"You notice their hands, how one pats the other?"

"I can picture how they straighten out each other's hair."

"You can see how they open and shut their purses, searching for Kleenex, handkerchiefs, snapshots?"

"I see them like they're standing right here beside us."

"One finally shuts up," Glen said, "and then she says, 'Dear, I'm embarrassed, but I can't remember your name.' The other one, she fiddles with the cuff on her jacket and touches her chin. She shuffles through pieces of paper she pulls out of her hand-bag, unfolds and reads a few and puts them away. She's not finding what she's looking for. She's on the verge of tears, but she smiles and she says, 'Oh, Dear, how soon do you need to know?'"

"God, Glen," Eddie said. "I should have seen that coming." He was laying in the background on the sign COUNT YOUR BLESSINGS. He planned to use three colors, purple, gold, and white, rectangle inside of rectangle inside of rectangle, all of it off-set on a gray panel. The words would be strung out on alphabet blocks, nothing ornate, but instead old manual-typewriter letters, each one twisted and angled along a line, tipped and turned and spun this way and that. Jumbled. Popsicle colors. Under the words, smaller blocks as if they had been tossed aside. There would be numbers on them. Your blessings. Count them. One, health. Two, family. Three, freedom. Four, five, six, seven.

Eddie stepped back. Sought distance. Your yonder point of view. He lit a Camel. BUCK UP was next. The pattern for the sign was laid out and cut. It left Eddie himself room to work in the abstract. He had designed a *B* angels would envy, this one flagged and embedded in geometry. He was using highlights and cast shadows, Tuscan block lettering, the ground a deep vermillion, the borders stippled lemon gold.

"Do you want to take a ride with me?" Eddie said to Glen. A sign was loaded in the truck, ready to post, one he had painted for a woman who ran a riding stable. "A couple of hours," Eddie said, "and we could get an early dinner. Bob Evans, my treat."

Glen said, "You want me to tag along?"

Maybe Glen's problem was the killer heat. Weeks of it now. People dying all over the Midwest, seven in Cincinnati this week. More in Chicago. The big cities like war zones. Temperatures in the triple digits. Heat index higher. Your sweat lay like a wrap on your arms. TV was now using the d-word. Drought. Maybe Glen's problem was the cicadas, a buzz that put doubts in your head. Most likely, it was the cancer. The mother of all dread. The balloon payment coming due. Whatever it was, Glen had not been leaving the house. He sat in his La-Z-Boy, the TV loud, soap operas on. CNN. He yelled at ESPN. *Base-*

ball isn't a sport. Hockey. Hockey? Soccer? For Christ's sake. What has happened to America?

His being here in the yard was a big step. Was a move away from his own fetid air.

"You could help me out," Eddie said. "One hour to the location. Ten minutes to put the sign in place, and then we eat."

Glen said, "Apprentice myself to you?"

"You know what I mean," Eddie said. "I'm offering you that free lunch they claim there isn't any of."

"Your mother put you up to this?" Glen glanced across the yard at Joy, who was watering her tomatoes. "You're asking an old man because you don't think an old man has anything to do. You got to keep the old busy or send them to daycare." Glen tapped his foot and said, "Put your right foot in, put your left foot in, and you shake it all about." He tried to shuffle his feet and he wobbled, almost hit the ground. "You do the hokey pokey," he said. Glen bent over and rubbed his leg. Massaged it. He said, "My damn leg belongs to someone else." He squeezed the thigh. Jiggled it. He said, "I'd say my dancing days are for the history books."

"I'm asking for the pleasure of your company," Eddie said.

"Horsefeathers, BS and my ass."

"Lunch is my treat."

"God save me from your treat," Glen said.

Good enough. Okay. Fine with Eddie. He located his keys and headed for the Toyota. He was driving out to Five Points, delivering the sign for Wandering Lakes, the riding stable run by a woman named Greta Bothers. Glen followed him, talking. He said, "I flew you out of Las Vegas over to the Grand

Canyon once when you were a baby." He zipped up the chest of his jumpsuit and said, "My Piper Cub. I sat you on pillows so you could see." He showed Eddie how high the stack was. He said, "The minute the plane took off, you fell asleep. We touched down, you woke up. You missed the whole flight. You slept through it coming and going."

Eddie said, "So you won't keep me company?"

Glen said, "I'm not talking about being company or not being company."

"You're saying I was missing what I was not supposed to miss, is that it?" Eddie said. "Is that what you're telling me?"

Their refrain. Give the boy a stick.

"Back when I was in Wyoming, when I was a kid," Glen said, "you were a sissy if you played the piano." He looked around at the Ohio woods. He blew a quick breath and said, "I wish I'd played the piano. I wish I'd broken all the rules."

"Will you come with me?" Eddie said.

Glen said, "Did I tell you I'm like the guy who was teaching his horse to live without eating?"

Eddie wanted to stamp a foot. Jump up and down. Do whatever it took to stop this. He said, "You didn't," and he hefted his toolbox into the bed of the truck. He wedged a tin of nails next to it. He tested the ropes on the sign and tucked in a corner of the tarp covering it. He turned to Glen.

Okay. Punchline.

Glen said, "The horse died before this fellow could finish the experiment."

One more dumb joke. Worse than the two-ladies bit.

A thumbs-up was all Eddie had to give. A pathetic gesture.

They both hated it and Eddie for being lamebrained enough to offer such a reward. A half-assed laugh would have been better. Was what was called for.

Bonding.

Too late.

Put the baseball mitts away. Let the air out of the football.

"You know what sad is," Glen said. "Sad is the fact that old men can't feed themselves."

Give it up, Eddie thought. You've sucked the subject dry, Glen. Old is old. Nobody able to stop it yet.

Eddie made sure he had extra rope in the truck. He counted cans of paint. Thinner. Brushes.

Glen said, "We can't get dressed by ourselves. Our belt buckles are tricky, and we twist our underwear so it's inside out. We put our pants on backwards. We spill food on us or leave it on our face. We have to ask for help so we can shit. You can't hurry the old, and if you do, it's stop and start, or stop and fart."

"Two hours," Eddie said. "An hour out. An hour back. Maybe Noah will join us for something to eat."

Glen raised his face to a plane splitting the sky, contrails up there like tic-tac-toe, and Eddie left him to his spot. He drove around the house and stopped in the driveway near Joy. She had finished watering the tomatoes and was standing by her wildflowers, the hose running at her feet. She kept her back to Eddie, was, he sensed, in tears.

He said, "Mom?"

Without turning, she said, "I'm being picked apart, Eddie. Nothing big. Nothing you can really complain about."

90   Darrell Spencer

"He's afraid."

"He's afraid?" Joy arranged the hose in the flowers. She walked over to Eddie, and she said, "You haven't heard his I'm-ready-to-meet-my-maker speech?"

Eddie had, more than once. It was the family theme song. Eddie said, "He's angry. He's scared. He's dying."

"He'll tell you he's not afraid."

"He is, though. Don't you think?"

Joy looked at the ground. Her lawn dry. Yellowed, stiff. She said, "Last night he tells me his being impotent is because of me. It's all my fault, every bit of it. He tells me you don't use it, you lose it. He says, im-*po*-tunt, like he's a stupid man. I'm the cause of the cancer. Things got backed up."

"He thinks that, he is stupid. He's more than stupid."

"I'm the one," she said. "He tells me I love to fight. I'm the one who's angry." She bent to pull a weed, but stood before she got it and said, "I don't recognize him. Where's the man I married?"

Eddie said, "He's what I always saw." Joy stared at him. She came closer, and Eddie got out of the truck. He said, "He was like a bomb in the house."

"I don't remember this. All the yelling he's doing now."

"He used silence."

"Yeah?"

"Yeah."

Eddie watched that sink in. He said, "You'd come to us. 'Your father,' you'd say, and then you'd tell us some complaint of his. There was something we had done he wasn't happy with. He didn't talk to us. He took you in the bedroom, and then he sent you out to tell us what was wrong while he lurked around outside or in the back of the house."

She said, "He did do that a lot." Joy moved her hose to a row of marigolds. They could see a yellow house on a hillside. It had red shutters. Not looking at Eddie, Joy said, "My heart is black and blue."

Eddie almost went to his knees.

"He makes me feel like prey," Joy said. "I'm on a short leash. I say the wrong word, or I don't say a word, and he tells me I'm waiting for him to die so I can find Mr. Right, like Mr. Right is double-parked around the corner. Where am I all day? I'm having affairs, he says. I'm seeing other men? At my age? He's lost his mind."

Eddie said, "I'm sorry."

Useless. *I'm sorry*—quintessential Eddie. You came to him for help and he hamstrung you and him. You might as well bay at the moon. Eddie's heart was in the right place. It felt and throbbed and hurt and bounced itself off the walls of his chest, and he could hold you tight and hug like a pro, but suggestion bumped against plan haplessly, gave up the chase, and slumped to the floor of his mind.

They heard Glen, who was yelling. "Same view from up here as it is down there." He was on the third-floor balcony. "Behave," Glen shouted.

Eddie had to go.

"Behave."

A dog far away began to bark.

Glen said, "I'm going to unzip. How much harm can I do?" He was loud. His shouting had the carry of a bullhorn.

Eddie said to Joy, "Do you want to come with me?"

She shook him off. She glanced at her watering.

"It'll be a drive," Eddie said. "We'll see some country. We can talk."

Glen yelled, and the dog kept barking. From somewhere in the trees, from the ridge in back of the house, a woman shouted. "Shut up, crazy man."

Glen barked. The dog barked.

"Putz," the woman yelled.

"I'm unzipping," Glen said. Louder. "I'm unzipping. I'm raising the dead."

Joy said to Eddie, "It's too much." She tugged her hose across the lawn to the flowers banked along the driveway. Now she couldn't see Glen, who was yelling, and the dog was barking.

How was Eddie going to describe this drive to M&M? In the sky, dead ahead, tracking toward its cave after one more day of service, was the sun. It was in his face. Couldn't be. It was three in the afternoon, and Eddie was driving east. Had to be, didn't he? West was the other way. No? He drove 682 along the Hocking and out of town. Caught 56. M&M wanted names and numbers. She studied the maps she downloaded, of the state, of the southeast part of the state, of Athens County, of Athens, The Plains, Nelsonville, Amesville. "You're on a road called Sweat Hollow and you don't know it?" she had said to Eddie on the phone one night. "Rum Ridge Road? Snorting Ridge

One Mile Past Dangerous Curve   93

Drive? Blackjack Ridge? You're losing your sense for details, Eddie. Take notes. You can write and drive. It's been done before." He crossed his heart. Swore an oath. In the future he would do better. His duty. Otherwise he hoped to die.

U.S. 56 torqued him through half-horseshoes and switch-backs. You learned to pay attention to the yellow signs up ahead and their black arrows telling you the turn thirty feet down the road was a doozy. To his left, a troop of wild turkeys hustled through a field of rolled hay. He pulled over and took a photo he would send to M&M. To his right, there was Fox Lake Road, then Salem Ridge Road, and a sign for Mud Lick Run. He scribbled the names on a yellow legal pad. Eddie was trying to keep his wheels on the asphalt, locate his compass, and take the notes M&M begged for. At a Y in 56 he hung a hasty left, worried he should have gone right, but knowing it would be okay. Now the sun was directly behind him. So, he was going east. Nope. Had to be west. No matter. There would be another road that would return him if he had gone wrong. A caution sign said LAND SLIDES, two words. There you go, Eddie thought, SHIT HAPPENS LAND SLIDES. Would make a great bumper sticker, a political slogan. Clinton could use it, take a shot at a third term in office.

Up Eddie went, then down, three roller-coaster hills, his stomach whooping, and then no sky where it ought to be. He was being funneled through woods, trees thick as corn in a field. Daylight, but dark. A creek beside the road was running clay red. Muddy. A truck passed coming the other way, and Eddie actually closed his eyes, there being no room to spare on the narrow two-lane. Eddie blinked, and there was the first sign he

94 Darrell Spencer

had painted for Cotton. CAN'T SLEEP? TRY TALKING TO THE SHEPHERD RATHER THAN COUNTING SHEEP. He emerged from the woods and found himself in the outskirts of Mineral, realized he *had* turned the wrong way. He parked on the grass lot of the Holiness Church and double-checked his map. His compass had disappeared, was not in the glove box, under the seat. Back or forward, didn't matter, road fed road which fed another road. Eddie could turn around or keep on trucking. He looked at the church, which was clapboard and no wider than a railroad car. Its backside had sat down like it was tired was all. There was an outhouse to the side next to a swing set.

He drove into Mineral itself, and it was like he had parted a curtain and entered a scary movie. The town dog was the rottweiler, five or six at each house or trailer, chained to fence posts, to steel rods. The town vehicle was your camouflaged truck, some kind of welded-together off-road machination. It looked like the place had been built overnight, like an army unit on the move. Men stood in groups, shit-kicking, back-slapping, grinning like jack-o-lanterns. Eddie rolled by, and they looked without looking and stopped their talking, as if he might overhear. Bit their tongues—you could see it. Eddie would tell M&M that if the Toyota had broken down he would have pushed it up the hill and beyond the city limits on his own, double-time, hoping for a downhill that could get him two or three miles' head start.

County 356 shuttled Eddie back to 56, which he stayed on until he got to Five Points Road. More over-hill-and-dale traveling. Deeper, thicker woods, then, snap your fingers, and right in your lap, a mowed field like you had drifted out of a theater

One Mile Past Dangerous Curve   95

in the afternoon and into sunlight. There would be a nice-looking home or a double-wide trailer squared-to on a piece of ground. Eddie's directions had him turning up a dirt road, which he did, only to find a cluster of trucks blocked his way in. Two dudes, sunning their shaved heads, were sitting out front in folding chairs like they were checking credentials. Both were drinking beer. One, using a hunting knife, was hacking at a stump. Whatever was going on was invitation only. Eddie backed out and drove off. At Five Points he passed three highway patrol cars motoring in the other direction. Law and order on its way. He took Dowler Ridge Road. Huntington was supposed to have set two posts in the ground exactly one half mile from the corner of Dowler and Buzzard Run.

The good news was the posts were in place. Huntington, true to his word, dug three-foot holes and cemented the bases. Eddie stuffed a wrench into his back pocket, juggled the four-by-eight duraply sign out of the truck bed, swung around and slanted it over one shoulder. It caught a breeze and almost twisted away from him. One end flew up, and the other end dropped. Seesawed. He steadied himself, recalibrated his feet. A beat-to-crap Chevy Impala cruised in close and parked crosswise. Eddie inched his way toward the posts, and a pickup, coming the other way, blocked the road at that end. He set the sign down and leaned it against the posts.

Incoming, Eddie thought. If this weren't the middle of nowhere, he would have said he was in a bad part of town.

A short dude, presence of a mailbox, demeanor of a trash can, got out of the Chevy. First thought Eddie had was that the man was his own nephew, that paw-paw had not wandered too far down the hallway in search of heat and a mate. Two of this guy's pals climbed from the backseat. One remained in the front, the passenger's side. No one left the truck. Its windows were tinted, smoky. The short guy's head was shaved, except for Elvis Presley sideburns flush to the top of his ears, the bottom stitched threadlike along his cheeks. He was wearing overalls and a gray, sleeveless sweatshirt.

"You done that?" he said to Eddie. He pointed at the sign.

Eddie assured him he had.

"Real fine work," he said.

Eddie was standing to the side of the road.

A guy hopped from the passenger side of the truck. He was tall, and moved like he was used to ducking. He was older than the rest of them. The engine idled. There were three or four men in the bed, one straddling the tailgate. No shirts on. The whole bunch of them making sure you noticed they were tattooed. All of them putting their ink on display. An ugly-as-sin kid—maybe fifteen—moved in next to the man who had spoken to Eddie and said, "Yeah yeah." On his face was hair yearning to be a beard. The young man was full of foul dumbass hope. No way would you want to spend time in close quarters with him. A bicycle chain shackled his wallet to his pants.

Eddie stooped for his sign and reached for the wrench, and a young kid—the third guy who had gotten out of the truck, who had circled around and sneaked in behind Eddie, out of Eddie's eyesight—said, "No, sir." He produced a gun and pointed it at Eddie's ear.

Jesus, Eddie thought. He had, one day at Canosa and Las

Vegas Boulevard, coming out of an AM/PM, been mugged and carjacked. Three in the afternoon. The good folks of Las Vegas drifting about nearby, pumping their gas, fetching their drinks and treats for their trips. Three dudes met Eddie at his car, one put a gun to Eddie's forehead, another slipped his hand in Eddie's back pocket and relieved him of his wallet, and the guy with the gun took the keys Eddie offered. Not a word had been said. Afterwards, Eddie sat on the curb and hoped he wouldn't pee his pants in front of the strangers who had gathered around. He fought off the dry heaves.

"I got twenty bucks on me," Eddie said.

Mailbox said, "We ain't thieves, boy."

Boy? Add five years to Eddie and he could be this youngster's father.

The tall guy who had climbed out of the truck told the dope with the gun to put it away. The idiot stuck it barrel-first down the front of his Levi's. The tall guy said to him, "Don't be doing that." He took the gun from him, and he said to Eddie, "We see your plates from Nevada, and we're curious about you being here in our state putting up this sign."

"I painted it," Eddie said.

"Someone hire you, did they?"

"The woman who owns the stables."

"We're not all that sure it adds to the beauty of our countryside," the tall guy said.

"Hell no," the gunslinger said. He reached over and took his pistol back. Held it barrel to the ground along his thigh.

"Yeah yeah," the kid said.

Eddie said, "You're telling the messenger is all."

Mailbox said, "What's he mean?"

"He's passing the buck," the tall guy said. "He is telling us he is the victim in all this. He's the poster boy for the way it is in America nowadays. No one willing to take responsibility for what they do." He had rehearsed what he was saying. It was the conversation he and his boys had while they sat around watching stock-car races. He walked over so he could take in the whole sign. Two teenagers were checking out Eddie's paint and equipment in the bed of the truck. One grabbed a gallon can of block-out white, and one of them opened Eddie's toolbox and selected a flathead screwdriver. He put it in his back pocket. Two others stayed in their truck, kept their backs to Eddie. One had a tattoo on his left shoulder blade. The other one, on his right shoulder blade. Eddie couldn't tell what they were of. Maybe birds. Hawks. Could have been words. Proclamations.

"Laws is laws," Mailbox said.

Eddie had no idea what he meant. Shit happens, Eddie thought. Land slides. The tall guy said to the kid who had pulled the gun, "Help him put that in place, will you, Henry?" Henry did, and Eddie bolted the duraply to the posts.

"You pay for assistance like this?" the tall guy said.

Eddie, threading a nut, said, "A guy did the posts, is that what you're talking about?" He wrenched the nut tight.

"Sort of," the tall guy said. He looked at the kid who had helped Eddie and said, "Henry, you feel compensated?"

Henry jerked, squinted like his eyes truly did hurt right this particular second. He was reaching far beyond craven. The kid didn't understand the word *compensated*. It was after him like a horsefly. He said, "No, sir."

One Mile Past Dangerous Curve   99

Fuck, Eddie thought.

"I got a desire for them shoes he's in," Henry said. He nudged Eddie's foot.

Mailbox said, "You all a long way from Nevada, boy."

"Yeah yeah," said the ugly kid.

The tall guy said, "The man did work for you, and he likes the shoes you got on."

"Yip," Mailbox said. "Yip."

Tall guy said, "You far from Nevada, boy. You in our territory. This whole state is private property to the likes of you."

Henry was scrawny and acting like he was about to be wormed. He was the color of dried weeds, had a beat-up face and the smudge of a mossy beard. Maybe ten random teeth. Those left were chipped and blued. His mouth was a hole. He was waving his pistol around.

"I asked you," the tall guy said to him, "to put that away. Take it to the car." Henry shoved it into his pants again.

Eddie flipped his wrench in the cab of his truck, and it bounced on the seat, hopped to the floor. He untied a shoe. One-hundred-fifty-dollar Nike cross-trainers. In a big city this could happen. In Las Vegas, in the middle of the day, at Canosa and Las Vegas Boulevard. It hadn't occurred to Eddie he would be mugged in the middle of the heartland, out here in all this green, nothing but trees laced with dogwood in bloom. Long tall purple flowers stretching in the sun. You go where people get robbed, you don't take your wallet, and you don't wear good shoes. You leave your expensive watch behind. You do the math. Eddie hadn't even considered the possibility of theft here in this mind-numbingly beautiful state. He untied his other shoe. He walked to the back of the truck and shut the tailgate. He put a foot on the bumper and jacked his shoe off. The other foot, the other shoe. He underhanded one to Henry, who whooped, struck by the glory of his own pea-brained thinking. Eddie tossed him the second shoe. Henry whooped. Did himself a hillbilly jig, like he was dancing at the end of a paddle.

Mailbox said, "Jesus, what pretty socks you wearing."

"So white, sign man."

"Blind you, them's so white."

"You use Tide, do you?"

"Bet they're brand-new."

"You got a mommy washes them for you?"

Eddie peeled off his socks and draped them over the side of the truck bed.

The teenager who found the screwdriver pried the lid off the gallon of white-out and lugged the can over to the tall guy, who said, "Do the honors." The kid flung the paint at the sign, swirled it across its face. His pal sloshed a second can on. Mailbox took the socks off the truck, and the tall guy said to Eddie, "We appreciate you hiring local labor. It's the American way. Think global. Buy local." He waved his hand and everyone headed for their vehicles. Only folk left were Eddie and the tall guy, who spit out of obligation to his badness and said, "You need more help, you let us know. Our number's in the book."

Eddie, sitting in the cab of the Toyota, checked the rearview, which featured the truck spinning its tires, hustling up dust, then turning full around. In the bed—he wasn't that sure, but because this had been in the back of his mind since they drove up—were Mark and Matthew, their heads shaved, each of them wearing a tattoo on a shoulder blade. Both sporting sunglasses. Eddie waited, then got out and wiped the sign clean. Tried thinner on his rag, but it didn't do much good. The lettering was left filmy, like it had already faded in the sun.

Nelsonville 8 miles. Eddie took the road. It had a name he didn't bother to write down. He wouldn't be reporting any of this to M&M. At an awkward bend that went up and then shot right, there at the top, was another sign he had painted for Cotton. It said THERE IS MERCY. THEN THERE IS MERCY.

Noah was not at the dealership. Only Olive Root. She located some work boots for Eddie, and he put them on without socks. He told her he had ruined his shoes in a muddy field. She didn't ask after the logic of his story—did he abandon them? step free and walk off?—and he didn't tell her what had happened or that he might have seen Noah's boys. Huntington had built Noah's sign, and Eddie set up to coat it out. The paint was quick-dry, and he planned to go ahead and lay in background colors before dark.

"Fruit in the season thereof," Olive Root said. She half sat on the hood of the Toyota, offering Eddie a banana she had peeled. He rolled paint. "I mean the body is real," Olive Root said.

God, Eddie prayed, put a sock in this woman's mouth.

She lugged her hair to one side, yakking. "With what we eat and getting our butts into exercise every day it's your health you're after," she said. "Ask anyone, even a child. Ask. Go ahead. Say to a child, 'What matters?' Today's kids know. Ask, say, what's the one thing you don't take a chance on? They'll tell you, because they teach these things in school as part of

102 Darrell Spencer

your educational package. The government requires it. Kids are under a lot of stress—guns, sex, AIDS, the kinds of things we never thought about. I didn't, at least. A six-year-old kid will tell you it's your health you're after. Your health is number one. A strong heart, blood pure as mountain springwater, lungs able to do what lungs do. Not to mention your colon."

The drive had not calmed Eddie down. The gun had been aimed at his head. The punks and the sign. His shoes. His socks. His feet, he knew, were going to blister in the boots which were too tight. The tops cut into his ankles.

"You won't use green, will you?" Olive Root said.

Eddie stroked on the final section of white-out. First coat.

Olive Root said, "You don't want to use green."

Noah pulled in and parked next to Eddie. Olive Root swayed, stepped away from Eddie's truck and said to Noah, "You don't want him to use green, right? We're in agreement on this." Stumped Noah. Eddie, at this minute, wasn't using green. He was rolling on another layer of block-out. There was no green in sight. Eddie shrugged.

"It's bad luck," Olive Root said. "You don't use green on a sign. You do and you're messing with the proper alignment of things."

Noah turned to Eddie, who kept rolling paint up and down the sign. A second coat. It would dry in fifteen minutes.

Olive Root said, "Don't listen to me." She bent herself into a stretch, highlighting her knees and elbows. She put herself sideways to Eddie and Noah and said, "No problem. This is no skin off my nose. I'm butting in. Color me silent. I'll just go ahead and close my mouth and take my lumps."

One Mile Past Dangerous Curve   103

Noah bummed a cigarette from Eddie. Frisked himself for a match. Olive Root said, "You don't see green on a motorcycle. You won't see any color of green on a motorcycle or a race car. You'll need to trust me on this. I dated a guy who raced flat track." She snatched the cigarette from Noah's lips.

"Hell's bells," Noah said.

Olive Root said, "Don't be a jackass." She tweaked the cigarette, and tobacco fluttered to the asphalt.

"What a nice thing for you to do," Noah said.

"As is always my way," she said. "I have your best interests at the center of my heart."

"You swooped in and saved my life."

"I did," she said. "I saved your life."

Noah said to Eddie, "Caffeine's out." Reports had come back from a doctor's visit. He said, "Cigs, out. Beer, whiskey, martinis. Stress." He raised hands to the heavens. "Stress. Like, what—it's a car coming at you?"

"His heart," Olive Root said, "is this close"—she pinched her finger to her thumb, tight, tips turning red—"to exploding."

Noah winced. "God," he said.

Olive Root said, "Bad luck's bad luck. You don't use green at a racetrack. You don't use green on a sign. You'll find truth is the root of all superstition."

Eddie looked to Noah.

She said, "You want to use green, don't let me stop you." She contorted herself into another stretch, other side, and she said, "Go ahead. But don't say I didn't tell you. I'm spindly, but I have backbone."

104 Darrell Spencer

"Green relates to lawns," Eddie said, and he immediately wished he hadn't. Talking to her was like singing at a freight train.

"Go with green. Test fate and the hand of God and all the other laws that govern the universe," she said, "and while you're at it, revise your wills. Update them. Better yet, phone your lawyers. You'll need to call in the sharks." She unbent herself and huffed off. "Put that in your pipe," she was saying. She stopped, turned and eyeballed Noah. She said, "And smoke it."

Noah told Eddie to do whatever they had planned. He said, "Eddie, we need to talk about Glen."

They arranged to meet down the road at the Dairy Queen for a burger. Eddie got there first, bought just a cup of coffee, and took a table. Noah arrived, Olive Root on his arm, like this was a French restaurant. She peeled off for the ladies room, and Noah passed a booth full of workers. One of them faked jerking off, and Noah said, "Keeping your minds busy." They all faked jerking off.

"Working hard, boys?" Noah said.

They cheered.

"Friends of yours?" Eddie said to Noah.

Noah said, "They do foundation and framing work." He went to the counter to order. He beat Olive Root back to the table and sat down. Eddie said, "I got mugged, only I'm not sure that's the right word for it."

"Someone robbed you?"

"Close to being a robbery." He showed Noah the boots Olive Root had given him. He described the trucks, the gun, the tall leader, the paint on the sign. Then he said, "I'm not sure but I think Mark and Matthew were with them. In the truck. Sitting in the bed."

Noah sat back. He said, "My boys?"

"I think so," Eddie said. "If so, they've shaved their heads clean as a whistle, and they've got tattoos on their backs. Whoever it was in the truck, they kept me from seeing their faces."

"Cigarette?" Noah said. He was right here in front of Eddie, but he wasn't seeing him. He said, "Jesus."

"You're not smoking," Eddie said.

"Shit," Noah said.

Eddie said, "I think it was them. I'd bet on it."

"Anything's possible." Noah told Eddie he heard Matthew and Mark had stayed in Ohio. He knew that much for sure. Had reports. But not one word from his boys. "Not even a postcard," he said, which was meant to be kind of funny but wasn't, not one little bit.

Eddie said, "Not even *send money*?"

"Can't joke about it," Noah said. "I got a truly bad feeling in my gut. This isn't going to be working out."

Olive Root sat down, the woman wearing wraparound sunglasses the color of grillwork. Serious hardware on her face. She collected a hunk of her hair at her forehead and stuck it high and to one side. Eddie said to her, "I can use any color you'd like." Peace, he was thinking, at any price. Whatever it took to shut her up.

"We'd like you not to use green," she said.

"What about blue?" Noah said. "Blue is a refreshing color."

Olive Root said to Noah, "Green is not bad luck. It's no luck."

Eddie said, "You want Snapper colors, right?"

"We don't want green," Olive Root said.

He said, "Snapper's red. It's Snapper red."

"No green. That's all I'm saying."

Noah's and Olive Root's numbers came up, and Noah went to get the food. Eddie measured the unfriendly part of himself at half an inch from flying this coop. Olive Root had the genius for getting under your skin. Irksome fit the lady to a T.

She, looking over her shoulder at Noah, said, "Doesn't Noah remind you of Elvis?"

"I don't see it," Eddie said. "Not enough hair, for one thing."

"With his beard, if you can imagine it," Olive Root said, and she wiggled her fingers near her face. "Put in your mind's eye Elvis and a beard on him." She covered her jaw and cheeks with her hands. She said, "Elvis grew a beard at one time, didn't he?"

Eddie said, "An Elvis sighting at the DQ."

"Come on. Noah in white leather," Olive Root said. "You can see a white scarf around his neck."

Noah returned. He handed Olive Root her food, and, sitting, he said, "Glen's worrying me."

"I can think of about thirty reasons," Eddie said. "Which are you narrowing in on?"

Noah said, "He bought the land for this place, and for the franchise down in West Virginia. For all four of them. Everything is only in his name legally. Me and him, we work off a handshake."

"He's your father."

"It's not 1940."

One Mile Past Dangerous Curve **107**

Eddie said, "I don't know what that means."

"What *what* means?" Noah said. "You don't know what that means? You're not stupid."

Eddie said, "It's your business. Yours and Glen's."

Olive Root jumped in. She said, "Glen fell off a roof once and angels caught him before he hit the ground."

"That's inspiring," Eddie said. "What are you saying?"

"They laid him gently on the grass like you would a baby."

"Glen needs to talk to Penrod," Noah said. "Penrod says we need to get all the legal stuff straight in case something goes wrong. Would you talk to him?"

Eddie said, "To Penrod?"

Noah said, "You're being an ass."

"To Glen. About land, the business. No, I won't talk to him."

"What if he loses his mind?"

"You mean goes more nuts than he already is?"

"I mean for real, not just old-man stuff, but certified insane. Put-away loony nuts."

Eddie said, "He's dying. He's not stupid or getting there."

"He's acting like he's losing it," Noah said.

Eddie said, "Noah. I'll do your signs. But that's it. You talk to him. Not me."

"I did. He won't talk about it. He gets up and walks out of the room. He takes his fucking camera outside and starts taking pictures of the bugs. Or he disappears completely."

"So take a hint."

"Take a hint? We're talking about a couple of million dollars here. We're talking my family's future."

Eddie said, "Your family's riding around in a pickup truck

robbing people." He had gone too far. He sat back, raised his hands. He was out of line, and he was admitting it. Was apologizing. He said, "Noah, it's not my business. I've never been part of it."

Noah said, "No one gets off that easy. The land gets tied up. It's family money down the drain."

"Gets off?"

"What about Joy?"

Eddie ate his response. His anger. He heard *Joy*, thought gloom. Heard *Joy*, thought of her black-and-blue heart.

Noah said, "Who knows what the courts will do with a certified crazy man, or if he drops over dead tomorrow? It's Joy's money. It's your money."

Not since Eddie was eighteen. Not since Eddie took a hike. His money was his money. Hadn't taken a dime from Glen.

"You know, say he wakes up only he doesn't wake up," Noah said. "Joy finds him gone."

"Gone?"

"Dead."

"Jesus, Noah."

"Don't blow me off."

"Cancer doesn't kill like that," Eddie said. "Cancer is never *you're here one minute, you're dead the next*. Cancer is slow and cruel."

"You don't know what he's done legally?"

Eddie raised his hands, saying, *Your problem*. Such was the posture his life took.

"It's Joy's problem," Noah said.

Eddie got up and walked out.

He caught a Phillies-Braves game at Lucky's on Court Street, and at eleven, back at the house, he came upon Glen asleep in front of the TV in a room off the kitchen. Eddie saw the light on and stopped on his way to the trailer. Glen was tipped back in his La-Z-Boy, balder, it seemed, than he had been earlier, like being so happened to him five minutes ago. He was wearing dark glasses. Twenty-nine dollars plus shipping and handling from Natural Vision USA. A month ago they arrived at the trailer, and Glen picked them up. One more item he didn't want Joy to know about. He showed them off to Eddie. The lenses were solid black plastic except for row after row of pinholes. You were supposed to wear them forty minutes a day, and, Natural Vision USA promised, you would improve your eyesight. Go ahead, their ads said, toss your bifocals in the trash. Throw away your contact lenses. So Glen, as if Joy didn't know, wore his in secret and took cod-liver oil pills for his retinas.

Eddie stood by his dad, the old guy whistling through his nose, his breathing difficult. Dying in his chair. Eddie fetched himself a beer, rattling bottles in the refrigerator. He heard Glen cough, then moan, and, walking out, passing by, he said to Glen, "You got twenty-twenty vision yet?"

Glen eased the glasses off and examined them.

"I'll see you in the morning," Eddie said.

Glen said, "Maybe you will. Maybe you won't." He placed the glasses on the end table and said, "I'll check the obituaries first thing and let you know." He shut the TV down.

God, one more fox trot. Another bit of Eddie and Glen tit-for-tat Eddie couldn't bear tonight. It was late. He had been robbed. He had been boomeranged by Olive Root and bush-whacked by Noah. His feet hurt. His ankles were probably bleeding. They were raw. Stinging. "You'll phone the morgue and ask them to see if you're on their list?" Eddie said.

Beat, shuffle, shuffle, beat. Beat, shuffle, beat. Their old routine.

Glen said, "I'll call the census bureau."

"I'm betting on you," Eddie said.

Glen lurched forward, jolted, then caught himself half a jerk before his head snapped off and thumped across the room. He rubbed his temples.

Eddie said, "Can I help you up?"

Glen, eyes wild, peeked at Eddie from between his fingers, and said, "Would you look at this? I've got this situation in my mouth." He opened wide, jutted out his jaw so his lower teeth showed.

"What am I looking for?" Eddie said.

"What about the teeth? Isn't there something strange going on?"

His teeth did crowd each other, were jammed together, too many people in this elevator. A car wreck, one of those chain-reaction crackups on a freeway. "What's happening to my mouth?" Glen said. His eyes—they looked like century-old bone china dug up and still caked with dried mud.

Eddie said, "Your teeth are okay."

Glen released himself deeper into his chair. He shook his head, discouraged, confused, like Eddie had tossed a frozen fish on a plate and served it to him raw here in the middle of the night. Glen said, "My brain, it gets bigger and bigger. You know how water does that to a sponge." He dropped his hands to his lap. "Tiny monkeys," he said, "they use sledgehammers and drive spikes into my skull from the inside out. Bone chips flying. Brain splatter. I keep thinking, *What about this? What about this?*"

Eddie crouched down and said, "Are you all right? Do you hurt somewhere?"

Glen said, "The operation was textbook, they tell me." He got up, stumbled. Eddie had heard it all before. Glen brushed against a lamp, rocked it on its base. He blinked and said to Eddie, "It's not something you can put into words. You can't tell someone else about it, not if you talked until the end of time." He staggered where he stood. Caught the back of a chair. He said, "I don't accept what they told me. The doctor botched it. I'll bet this house on that. Some fool screwed up. Something happened when I was under the knife, so I got this feeling I can't pin down, and I think it did something to my hearing." He bowed his head. "Not the way to run a railroad," he said.

"You're worried?" Eddie said.

"It doesn't hurt," Glen said. "And I pee me a river. But you can't have them do that to you and be normal afterwards. Too much is going on down in that area."

Eddie wondered if Glen comprehended the diagnosis. If he understood that there was nothing to do to stop the cancer. It had spread before they took his balls. He was dying.

To be told you're dying—no way could Eddie get a handle on that kind of news. Wish upon a star—yeah, there's a tune for you. Roll the credits.

Glen said, "You're not who you were. Not after that."

Eddie stood. He said, "Can I help?"

"I'm not worried about meeting my maker," Glen said. "I'm lying in bed at night, and I'm hearing a thousand people talking to me. They have good things to say. They're waiting for me. My mother, my father, Mr. Highway himself—they visit. They talk like we're talking here, you and me. Clear as a bell. Real as my shoes. They're in the room with me and they are big as life."

"No wonder you're not sleeping," Eddie said.

Glen took stock of his own hands, his knees, his bad leg. Then he said, "One day, I was standing near the canal— maybe I was swimming, I don't know. This would be in Spanish Fork, there in Utah. I'm standing on the ground, on a fire road, and the apple trees were in blossom, so it was spring. There was nothing but white and pink and red as far as you could see. Trees in rows. Row after row. That orchard was as wide as you can imagine. It went all the way from the hills to the old highway. I don't know what I was doing, if I was swimming or just horsing around, and I had this feeling come over me. It wasn't a bad feeling, only it was full of sorrow that made my bones ache. I didn't sob, but if I had done anything like that, *sob* would have been the word you'd use for it. Something was inside of me trying to get out. I could see my mother and Mr. Highway talking on the back porch of our house, and I wanted everything to always be the way it was at that moment. I wanted time itself to stop and leave us alone. I was twelve years old. Maybe thirteen at the most. We moved before the year was over. Mr. Highway and Clara wore their religion on their sleeves, so up there by the canal I got on my knees in the dirt, and I prayed that time would stop. Right there under the sky—the middle of the day—I asked God to do one simple thing, to leave us alone. Not a big request. Leave us alone was all I said. I wanted things to stay the way they were. I was a kid, and I didn't think that was too much to ask for."

It was two A.M. in Ohio. Eleven P.M. in Nevada. Eddie said to Maggie, "It's Wednesday here and Tuesday where you are." M&M was too old and wise to be impressed. He described Mineral, the wrongheaded turns he had taken, the exfoliating green that hung and spread and climbed and tunneled, the narrow two-lanes that tossed and turned you.

Next to him on the redwood table were pots of morning glory. Eddie knew the colors by heart. Chrome red. Fuchsia. Coral. Scarlet. Cicadas, on the flowers, on the ground, on the table, were shedding their shells. Roscoe was absent, and Eddie was missing him.

Eddie left out the robbery or mugging or whatever it was.

He told Maggie that he was standing on Dowler Ridge Road, admiring his work, the sign he had done for Wandering Ponds and Mrs. Greta Bothers—actually he had just wiped off what he could of the white-out from the surface—and nine—yeah, he counted them—nine Canada geese flew over so low, had he tried, he could have jumped up and snagged one. It was so quiet he heard their wings flap.

M&M said, "Did they honk?"

"No need to," Eddie said.

She said, "No traffic, right?"

"No traffic."

Oh God, he thought. M&M. One more joke. One more song. One more brick in the seawall.

Maggie was eleven when Eddie went to her dance studio to drive her home. She wasn't quite done. Eddie sat sideways in a chair made for a small child. M&M was wearing tights under gym shorts. On top, a white t-shirt. She walked to a spot across the room, kitty-corner to Eddie, and before she began to dance, she crossed her braids so that she could take them into her mouth, so that she could bite down on them. She held them there, and she began to move.

She doesn't want them to whack her, Eddie thought. It's so they won't whack her in the face.

Cotton, dressed in white slacks and blue blazer, did a quick sad little soft-shoe. He needed only a straw hat, one of those hoofers wore in old flicks. He said, "Foos. Balls of fire in the sky. The pilots saw them—the foo fighters. From every country, and not only the pilots, but whole air crews. The radar watchers. Soldiers on the ground. World War number two. The war that didn't end all wars. The Air Force, the Army, the Navy, every nation that was involved—no one could say what it was they were seeing. Russian pilots. Japanese pilots. Germans. Our own. The government was clueless. We thought the Nazis had a secret weapon. The Nazis were sure we did. Then we accused the Japanese. They thought it was us. Both sides were being stalked by the foos. Zippy airships out of nowhere, here, then gone in a flash. There are photographs."

"UFOs?" Eddie said.

"There is, was, never has been any official determination other than the usual. Johnny Pilot is out of step. Johnny at the Radar is seeing what isn't really there." Cotton circled a finger at his ear and said, "Johnny is crazy." He sipped his drink. He said, "That was your government's answer."

Eddie said, "They called them foos?"

"Where there's foo there's fire is what the saying was," Cotton said. He kept that tap dance going in his knees. He said, "Common sense tells you there's got to be life smarter than we've got going for us on this planet."

Eddie said, "Glen tells me all I have to do is look up."

Cotton said, "All anybody has to do is stop long enough to check their surroundings and to think for a minute and a half."

A.J. said, "Your own thoughts are running deep, Pop."

Cotton said, "I know things."

"You do, you do," A.J. said.

"I have seen some stuff," Cotton said.

"Amen," A.J. said. "Amen."

"My kid," Cotton said, "the smart-ass."

Eddie had to go. He and A.J. had spent the last two days in Columbus. Diana Krall concert one night, Eddie's idea of singing. German Village the next day. They stopped at an Amish shop on the return trip and bought Cotton a bench. Then they swung by Eddie's and collected one more of Cotton's signs. A.J. met Joy. Said hello to a mute Glen, the man not taking his eyes off the soap opera he was badmouthing. KINDNESS, Cotton's sign said, IS A LANGUAGE THE BLIND CAN SEE AND THE DEAF CAN HEAR, allegro lettering, looped and eared.

Flourishes stuttering above and below the words. All of it foregrounded by a lavender panel. Cotton paid Eddie a bonus and was winking, he felt so good about what he was seeing here on the four-by-eight duraply. He pronounced the sign perfect. He dug a pen knife out of his pocket and said, "Mumblety-peg?"

Eddie said, "Got to go."

"Lord got to love you, Eddie," Cotton said.

"Stick around," A.J. said. "We'll make a pizza run."

Eddie said, "I better not."

"Not because of me, I hope," Cotton said to Eddie. "Your leaving, I mean. Not my fault. It's early. We'll have dinner helicoptered in. What else do you two have to do on a Tuesday night in Ohio? Go for a swim. There's water. You folks are young. Stick around for the bullfrog concert. Have sex."

A.J. said, "You're feeling your oats, Pop."

"What? Is there some reason not to?" Cotton tested his footing. He said, "Is Eddie married? You kids have condoms?" Here in front of Eddie was a man who knew how to jump up and down in the world. "If not," Cotton said, "I do."

One week later. The flyer called it an Absolute Auction. It was Open to the Public, the sale of the trust and estate of the late Hazel Wheelwright, who lived in her lovely country home for sixty-three years, the last ten with her spinster sister, Cornellia. All items must be sold in one day. There were buildings full to the brim, every nook and cranny—a large two-story farmhouse, a garage, barn and sheds, a machine shop, chicken coops, potato cellar. The flyer listed furniture, major appliances, antiques and collectibles, pottery, glassware, guns and a gun cabinet. Over seven hundred salt and pepper shakers. Fifteen hundred postcards. Grossman Rockwell figurines. *Saturday Evening Post* covers—"Summertime," "Love Letter," "The Diary," "Runaway Pants." Day Lily china. Depression-era glassware. A mission-oak drop-front writing desk w/pigeon holes in need of repair. A stove and a turn-of-the-century safe. The auctioneers were Mr. Ottie Opperman and Mr. David Flood. They were selling, for the estate, a 1985 Chevy Custom Deluxe-10 pickup, automatic, eight-foot bed with top, only thirty-five thousand miles on it. There was a mint-condition Dodge Dart to be sold. A cement mixer had to go. Two farm tractors, a John Deere "M" with Touch-O-Matic Hyd. controls and a good I.H. Cub tractor with wide front.

"So, are you coming or not?" A.J. said to Eddie.

Eddie's idea of an auction was your sitcom situation where they took your bid if you scratched that itch on your cheek, and he had seen two minutes on the national news, Sotheby's selling Van Goghs, highbrow and highfalutin, all of it—the dinner-at-eight clothes, the dealers, the priggish rich sitting in rows. Something clandestine in everybody's stance. Furtive. Bidders on telephones, their toadies roaming about and double-checking how far the buyer would go. One-hundred-dollar full-color programs, not the goldenrod, Kinko's-printed flyer Eddie held in his hand.

"The sun's shining. We'll be outside," A.J. said. "It'll be rowdy." She led Eddie to his truck.

Which meant another drive he would record in his head and

118   Darrell Spencer

eventually play back for M&M, tell her how the string-like roads threaded them into and out of woods and past open fields, how he raced up, over and down the hills, their lift and fall in his stomach. He would re-create the whoop and holler of it for her. The Wheelwright farm, the flyer claimed, was easy to find, if you turned off I-33 at Route 595 and drove east, as if you were going to New Straitsville, only once you got there you took the right-hand leg of the T-stop in the middle of town, this side of Casey's grocery, and kept going on to Shawnee, where you looked for the new Conoco on 93. Half a mile beyond, you turned onto Blackjack Hollow Road, which became Goat Run–Honeysuckle Road, then Wheelwright Ridge Road, and it was under a mile you traveled to the farm.

Nothing but two-lane, Eddie pictured himself on the phone telling M&M, trying to think of a comparison, of a place they had been together. The drive to Lake Mead if you drove through Boulder City? Nope. Not the same kind of loneliness. The road south out of Las Vegas if you were headed for Search-light? Nah. Not quite. An altogether different kind of vacant. He couldn't come up with one adequate comparison. Or the exact word. *Hell-bent* almost fit. Twisty. Kinked. Coiled. Roads, he would say, ad hoc and iffy. Turns like a quick fix, ones a horse on a gallop might have made without too much trouble 150 years ago. *I'm downshifting so much I'm getting Pop-eye arms*, he would tell her. He wasn't sure he could explain the fog-like mist that hung above the land in the middle of the day. He would tell her about the sign they saw for a yard sale. *Keep Going You're Getting There 1 More Mile Past Dangerous Curve*, which lived up to its billing, which was a yank and a prayer to

One Mile Past Dangerous Curve   119

your left. Eddie slowed to fifteen and still nicked the soft-shoulder. Pitched A.J. into the door. The lady running the sale, sitting on a couch in her front yard, a cigarette held like her ear was smoking it, waved to them, a cat on her lap, three black dogs asleep in the shade cast by a rusted-out Pontiac whose trunk was strapped shut.

Driving the circles into hell, Eddie might say. Like one of those open-pit copper mines.

And M&M might say, Down and down we go.

Eddie and A.J. turned south on what would have been 93 had they gone north, but was 155, and they reached Hemlock before A.J. convinced Eddie to turn around. Sure enough, returning the way they had come, they saw the Conoco. There was a sign: AUCTION TODAY. Then they found Blackjack Hollow, which devolved into dirt-and-gravel Goat Run–Honeysuckle, and finally Wheelwright Ridge, tree limbs arching overhead, no sunlight piercing the leaves. Eddie, directed by more signs, parked in a field. The place was packed, like a drive-in movie. Trucks, vans, station wagons. Lots of Plymouths and Chevys from the sixties and seventies, their chrome gone missing or hanging by a thread, rust eating at their doors, their windshield wipers bent against themselves. Cars that made Eddie think of vintage ashtrays.

In the shade, in a grove of trees, were Amish buggies, the horses unharnessed and nibbling grass, shaking flies off. Two straw-bent young men wearing those saw-blade beards and round-as-a-throw-rug hats sat on the back of a buggy, kicking their legs like five-year-olds. There was a woman in the seat, cloaked, as if the temperature were forty, not eighty-five and climbing. Bonneted. She was selling butter and eggs. The men were drinking Coca-Cola and eating pie. There was a product placement for you. Coke would pay a fortune for this picture. *Even the Amish can't resist the pleasure of Coca-Cola.*

"I'd say we're going to a party," Eddie said to A.J. They were walking through red clay and stubble and dodging cicadas. "Something like Halloween."

A.J. said, "You'll see."

"Maybe a hay ride?" he said.

Eddie heard the auctioneer in the distance, the way you picked up the PA announcer if you lived in a neighborhood where a football game was being played.

Ottie Opperman, a guy who had some Little Richard in him, some Elvis, some Conway Twitty—his voice, the sway of his arms, there in the hips and one bouncy leg—he stood on the flat bed of a wagon, and a crowd surrounded him, five, six people deep. Most everybody stood, but squatters had settled on furniture that was up for sale, on stools, couches, dining-table chairs. Others brought along their own canvas-back fold-out seats. Three solid-looking citizens sat on a tractor tire that had been painted white and turned into a planter for pansies. People were sitting on boxes. A.J. saw a friend and said to Eddie, "Back in a minute."

He couldn't follow the bidding. It carried on, had its own music and logic and arithmetic. Few people, other than the bidders on an item, listened. People chatted, joked. One woman scribbled at a crossword puzzle. Another lady in pink was embroidering. At the edges of the yard, the smokers puffed away and choreographed their footwork. Eddie joined them

One Mile Past Dangerous Curve   121

and got a Camel going. A corn-fed kid wearing an Ohio State cap and t-shirt clapped a guy on the shoulder and said, "I heard you getting loud out by the barn, and I thought you was a cussin'."

"A cousin?" the man said.

"Well, that too," Ohio State said, and he pumped the man's hand, saying, "A cussin', and I was about to join you."

Eddie caught the tail end of a joke, a guy saying, "If it's got tits or wheels, sooner or later it'll be a problem."

It was a square dance, men and women side-stepping each other, checking out items that were stacked on plywood tables on top of sawhorses. No way Ottie and his pal would be able to sell it all in a day. It couldn't be done. There must have been thirty boxes full of glasses alone. There was crystal and a full set of Honeymooner mugs. The flyer said they were selling seventy silver dollars one at a time. Eddie was thinking it would take weeks. No one could talk and exchange money fast enough to get this done while there was still daylight. There was a neon sign for Budweiser. One table held nothing but pots and pans.

"We'll take bidder's choice on these miner's lamps," Opperman was saying. "We got bidder's choice on the lamps." The first one went for fifteen dollars. Then more lamps, ten bucks each, and finally one last lamp for five.

A.J. stopped by, told Eddie she was going to get a number and look around. He decided he would stay put, and she was gone, headed toward a barn. Opperman shut down the bidding on a pressure cooker, brand-new, never been out of its box. He said, "You bought it. Right there. A thirty-dollar bill." He got the buyer's number. "Number 107, number 107," he said. A woman, chewing gum, sitting at his side, recorded who was buying what. Opperman said, "You got a bargain, friend. Best buy today." The buyer's number, printed on a card, was curled and curved to fit to the crown of his cap above the bill. He wore a t-shirt that said *The Great Indoorsman*. Opperman sold six chairs by the piece, six times the money. Next up was a book, *ABC's of the Human Body*.

Eddie lit a Camel off his first one, and here was Huntington Bark at his elbow. "Hey," Huntington said. He gave Eddie his hand, and they shook like a pair of bankers with gout. Huntington had grown a mustache, one he curled at the tips. He was wearing mustard-colored overalls, the kind mechanics used to work in. His shirt was red, and he had wrapped a red scarf around his neck.

"That's no sale," Opperman said. "No sale. We'll try it again later." He handed the book to a helper and said, "We got some picture frames. Victorian. Who'll give me fifty?" He described them. Oak, he thought. Gilded. In terrific shape. One of his ring men held two of them high above his head and turned in a small circle. Opperman said, "You're buying all of them. Who'll give me forty? Thirty?" Huntington asked if Eddie was here for a reason, and Eddie said he was just being a sidekick. He told Huntington about A.J. and pointed her out.

"The woman," Eddie said, "at Cotton's."

A.J. was talking to a lady in floppy black hat, a lady wearing a shawl and leaning on a walking stick. "I've seen her before," Huntington said of A.J. "She comes to these."

Eddie said, "She tells me what she's after is a good time."

Huntington nodded, said, "So she's the one at Cotton's?"

One Mile Past Dangerous Curve 123

"She is," Eddie said. "One of his daughters."

Huntington said, "I'd say that might put the lie to what's being rumored around."

Eddie said, "Except in the hands of gossips and lawyers."

"She's good-looking."

Eddie huffed smoke and saw, through it, the tall guy who had robbed him. His was not a face Eddie was going to forget. The man had one of those noses shaped like sliced apple. His hair, stiff, unlovable, was big-time fifties hood. You could see where the words *duck-ass hair* came from. He was wearing a satin jacket, crimson, Ohio State on the back. Eddie nodded toward the man and said to Huntington, "You know that guy?"

Huntington didn't.

"You haven't seen him around?"

"I might have. You know how that goes."

Eddie took a drag and said, "You after anything particular?"

"The tin," he said. "You know, toys and the like." He had set a couple of cardboard boxes at his feet. Toys in them. He showed Eddie a few he had bought, a Buddy L Kennel truck, a bulldozer, which was missing parts. He had paid six hundred for a G-Man Pursuit car. Mint. Huntington told Eddie he had been ready to go to a thousand dollars if he had to. Made Eddie wonder how crazy the world had actually become. Made him question when evolution had put itself in reverse. You got kids dying because there's no food or penicillin or their mom gave them AIDS. You got sports and its fools refusing to play a game if they don't make twelve million more than last week's star. And you got a handyman in Ohio willing to pay a thousand dollars for a tin car. Huntington stowed his loot in one of the boxes. He said, "I can clear fifty or sixty bucks on the Buddy L over in Marietta." But he wouldn't sell the G-Man car for the price of a new house. He had been three years hunting one down.

The guy who robbed Eddie bid on a rifle. A white tag hung off its barrel. The man kept moving, nitpicking his way through the crowd, spying over shoulders, handshaking people, giving everyone his charm and a big grin, catching the bid in time to up it. He was acting like his going after the rifle was secondary to everything else he was doing on the planet. Hell, he was here by accident and might as well spend a few bucks. The price reached nine hundred.

Eddie said to Huntington, "Nine hundred?"

"It's worth every penny," Huntington said. "That's Civil War."

Eddie raised his hand to bid. Opperman said, "One thousand." That was easy. Thirty seconds of Opperman's song, and the price was fifteen hundred. The robber had high bid.

Huntington said, "That's about what it's worth."

Eddie bid again. Sixteen hundred. Two other men drove it to eighteen. Eddie's robber bumped the price to two thousand, and Eddie went to twenty-one hundred. Huntington spun on his heels and stepped away from Eddie, like he was making sure he wasn't seen as a party to this, like he was about to see a car wreck he couldn't stop. Then he was back at Eddie's side. Not wanting to miss the fun. The robber bid twenty-three, Eddie twenty-four. Twenty-five. Twenty-six. Twenty-seven, and Eddie quit, stepped on his cigarette butt and walked away. The guy collected the rifle, which he hauled around behind the barn.

One Mile Past Dangerous Curve   125

Huntington took off for the parking field. He wanted to unload his boxes and lock up what he had bought so far.

"Hey, hey, mama," Opperman sang, "won't you come out tonight." One of his spotters, down in front, held up a coffee table. "Fifty. Who'll give me fifty," Opperman said. Nothing. No takers. "I need forty," he said. "Thirty, thirty-five." Someone jumped in at twenty, and the price quickly leapfrogged, at one point Opperman saying, "Sicky-five, sicky-five, sicky-five. Got sicky-five, need seventy." Price rose to one hundred. A man and a woman—he was to Opperman's left, she was to his right—they got in a tug-of-war. The man was dressed like he had dropped by on his way home from his job changing tires on semis. The woman was determined in her sweatpants and a baseball cap. Opperman's helper, keeping the coffee table aloft, focused on the man, said, "Got it," when he bid, which amounted to the man clawing at the air. The woman nodded her bids. At one point there was some confusion, and Opperman said to his helper, "I'm with you, Harry. I'm with you at one-fifty. I got one-fifty, need one-sicky." He flicked his hand at the woman, the gesture saying, *Are you in?* She made a cutting motion chest high, and Opperman said, "One-fifty-five. I've got one-fifty-five, need one-sicky." His helper, egging the man on, said to Opperman, "You got it." Opperman turned toward the woman. "It's Amish," he said. "The real McCoy." A bid came from behind him, and he spun around, almost toppled, righted himself, and said, "Don't try that at home, folks." Then it was over, the table going for three hundred bucks. Opperman said to a guy sitting in the back, "Couldn't tell if you was bidding or swatting bugs." The

126 Darrell Spencer

cicadas electrified the trees. They flung themselves into and through the crowd. Not buglike. Heavier. Noisier. On their own irksome lark. A little of the practical joker in them. Eddie watched a man pick one from a woman's hair and hold it up for her to see. Eddie felt one on his neck and knocked it off. He spotted A.J. inspecting an armoire. It was grouped with a ladder-back chair and a sofa. He moseyed over and said, "You got your eye on that?"

Behind Eddie, Opperman said, "We've got an announcement." Eddie turned around. Opperman reached down, shook a woman's hand, and said, "Good to see you." She moved on, and Opperman read from a note he had been handed. "Steve," he said, "your cattle are loose. One bull plus cows. You need to go shut your gate."

"The armoire's sold," A.J. said to Eddie. Then she led him over to an iron bed. They passed two farmers talking about stretch vases like they were in a field of rolled hay dithering over the weather, lamenting the drought that had settled in. "Can we get that in your truck?" A.J. said to Eddie. The bed was gorgeous and simple.

Sure. No problem. The frame broke down. It would fit.

"I'm going for it," she said.

The bed was near the man who had robbed Eddie. Eddie listened to him talking to a guy who most likely played Santa Claus at Christmas. The man had the beard and the belly for the job. The rifle was a Spenser.

A.J. wandered off, and Eddie sat on a bench. He was there, lighting a Camel, when his robber hunkered down next to him and said, "I know you from somewhere?"

One Mile Past Dangerous Curve 127

Eddie finished getting his cigarette going. He cut the man a look. Blew smoke.

"We met?" the man said. He put out a hand to shake, and Eddie ignored it.

Eddie said, "It's always possible. You know how they talk about this being a small world."

The guy was rubbing at the rifle's stock. He said, "Carbine, but you know that, right? Not your everyday rifle."

Eddie inhaled.

"You know what I mean?" the guy said.

"I don't," Eddie said. "A gun's a gun."

"It's a rifle."

"Right. A gun's a gun."

"You was in there bidding, wanting it," the man said.

Eddie said, "Not me." He allowed smoke to drift free. He said, "I got twenty dollars in my pocket and less in the bank."

"You wasn't bidding?"

"I don't even know how."

"You raised your hand."

"Is that all you have to do to bid?" Eddie said. "Maybe I was swatting bugs. That's a real possibility."

"I was thinking I saw you."

"I don't have a number," Eddie said. He showed innocent hands like he had washed them two seconds ago in exactly the way his mommy had taught him. You know. You soap and you suds and you wring and you hum the birthday song. Song's done, so are you. Eddie made a big production of checking all his pockets.

The guy stood up, and Eddie stared at the auctioneer. He

was a new one, was the difference between country and easy-listening, Johnny Cash vs. one of the Everly Brothers. Opperman introduced him as Mr. David Flood.

"America's heritage," the robber said. He held the rifle at arm's length, like he was about to rack it on a wall. The man was truly in love with his purchase. His boots were snakeskin, and in slots on a leather harness strap around each heal, he had stuck silver bullets.

Eddie said, "You're talking to the wrong guy. I don't know the first thing about that gun."

"American know-how," the man said. "One of the first repeaters. Americans showing the world how Americans can figure things out. We go everyone else one better."

Eddie said, "There's a small view of the universe."

"Truth is truth."

"If you say so."

The man said, "This is the rifle Lincoln ordered for the Union soldiers."

Eddie said, "Now there I think you got that wrong."

"It's history," the man said. "You can read about it."

"If you say so."

The guy cradled the rifle against his stomach and said, "You say you're not from here?"

"Nevada," Eddie said.

"Nevada's a long ways off."

"You look at my truck you'll see Nevada plates on it."

"I'm believing you."

"You think we might have met in Nevada?" Eddie said. He got to his feet. "Maybe we ran into each other in a casino?

Maybe you had some boys with you? There is a chance of that, of us meeting in Las Vegas. Everybody's been to Las Vegas. A man like you, I'm sure you have. So we could have run into each other. You think so?"

"That didn't happen."

"It's not a possibility you want to entertain?"

"Never been there."

"You haven't? That makes me sad," Eddie said. "It's pretty out there. Not like here at all."

The guy said, "You a Jew boy?" He said it like he meant no offense. Like he was hunting facts was all. Like he had practiced saying the words.

Eddie said, "There's an even narrower view of things."

"What does that mean?"

Eddie said, "Did you want something?"

"I didn't," the man said. "It's friendly circumstances, all these people coming together, and I was doing what I could to contribute to the atmosphere, plus there was me thinking I'd met you somewhere before, like you knew someone I knew, and I wasn't wanting to ignore that possibility. I didn't want to be unfriendly in case we was acquainted. Courtesy being one of the building blocks of civilization as we understand it in the twentieth century. You learn that in kindergarten. You can be assured I wasn't intending any aggravation on my part if that's what has occurred."

"For who?" Eddie said.

The guy said, "So you wasn't bidding?"

"If I was, it was for fun," Eddie said. "You know, as an experience. So I could feel a part of the atmosphere, the circumstances, as you say. I was killing time. Being my own kind of friendly."

The robber ducked his head.

Eddie said, "I guess you could say it was kind of a joke on my part." He let smoke escape, and the guy walked away, direction of the parking field, looking like he was leaving. He stopped, went to one knee, and aimed the rifle at cows bunched under a tree on a hillside. Overhead vultures circled. All of it as if one of your big-time assholes had staged the scene.

A couple of hours later A.J. outbid a farmer and paid for her bed, and Huntington helped them break it down and load it into the truck. He sidetracked Eddie on the way back to the auction, saying he had something to show him, but said, instead, "He's bad news."

Nothing Eddie didn't already know. He said, "How bad?"

"I didn't ask. Got the sense God gave me." He put a finger to his lips. Shush. Don't say a word. "You know how it is," Huntington said. "If it ain't your business, don't be asking the price."

Eddie wondered if the man had a name.

"Calls himself Kefauver," Huntington said. "You know that's got to be a lie."

Eddie caught up with A.J. circling around the backside of the barn. She saw a lamp she wanted, but they had missed a chance at it when they were loading the bed in the truck. The United Methodist Church had set up a tent and was selling homemade pie and soda pop. Cookies. Hot dogs. Sloppy joes. A.J. bought Eddie a piece of blueberry pie and a Coke. She bid on, but didn't get, a set of Yogi Bear TV trays.

In the truck, on their way out, she said, "So, a good time was

One Mile Past Dangerous Curve   **131**

had by all?" It was then, bumping through the field, Eddie told her about the man, the sign, his shoes, the robbery, and she said, "You're sure it was the same person."

Eddie crossed his heart and said, "Oh, I am."

"But he didn't recognize you?"

"I think he did. I don't know. He's in some kind of role, living out the movie of his life." The truck caught a rut and shot left. Spun mud getting back on track. Eddie said, "He wasn't playing a game. He was pissed I'd bid. Maybe he didn't remember me."

"You sure?"

"I was thinking he'd remember the plates. The Nevada part of all this. He didn't forget that."

"So he did know who you are?"

"Or figured it out quick."

"A real jackass," A.J. said.

Eddie said, "You win the understatement of the year award."

And there the man was, standing by his own truck, lifting, as an adios, a cap he had donned. He had one gold tooth right in front. There was a chest of drawers in his truck bed. Next to it, a coat rack.

A.J. said, "What'd your friend say about him?"

"That he's bad news."

"This you already experienced," she said.

Eddie had.

A.J. unwrapped tissue paper from around a brass dish she bought for him. It said POCKET CHANGE across the top.

He said, "You bought that for me?"

She said, "A place for you to park your money at night."

The new sign said FIGHT TRUTH DECAY / BRUSH UP ON YOUR BIBLE DAILY. Cotton and Eddie, their usual Rolling Rock in hand, sat on Cotton's porch. A.J. was inside. Eddie had used Colgate colors and lettering, and he abandoned the ornate first letter. Cotton was pleased. He saw that form had followed function, or some such thing.

Ohio was sticky. The U.S. was hot coast to coast. More folks reported dead in Chicago. The old. The shut-ins. The sick. The poor dying in Louisiana. In Texas you weren't supposed to go outside.

It was evening, and Cotton's bullfrogs sounded like they were moaning. The cicadas had ceased their torture for the day.

Eddie told Cotton the details about the robbery. He described the guy at the auction. Kefauver.

Cotton said, "Tattoos, you say?"

Eddie said, "Some."

"All the same?"

"I didn't notice."

"Shaved heads?"

"Not Kefauver, who seemed to be speaking for everyone else."

"But the others?"

"Some of them, they had hair. One didn't for sure. You think you'd remember exactly, but I don't."

"Your brother's boys were with them?"

"I'd bet on it."

Cotton stood and walked over to the sign, squatted right in front of it. "You do profoundly fine work," he said. "What's the trick with the corners?" He touched the foot of the Y in DAILY. "So sharp," he said. "Like a machine not a person did them. People suffer from too many imperfections to be painting corners like that."

"A trade secret," Eddie said.

Cotton said, "You tell me and you have to cut off my hands?"

"Exactly."

A.J. opened the front door, leaned through it, and said, "You two enjoying the weather?"

Eddie patted the porch for her to sit down.

She said, "I'm staying where it's cool."

Cotton retreated to the shade. He said, "You might have been dealing with hilljacks. A bunch of Ohio boys who think they're outlaws. There's every chance under the sun they're growing pot near where you were." He stepped over, reached for Eddie and helped him to his feet, saying, "Were there cornfields in the area?"

Eddie hadn't noticed.

Cotton said, "It could have been pot. It could have been good old boys restless and feeling nasty. It could be skinheads. There are pockets of them here. There's no question about that."

"Nasty is giving them too much credit."

"One more minute out here," Cotton said, "and I'll faint. Come in? I'll make some phone calls."

Inside Cotton gave Eddie three-by-five cards for the next three signs. One said, IF YOU'RE HEADED THE WRONG WAY /

REMEMBER GOD ALLOWS U-TURNS. Cotton said, "I'm thinking of limericks."

"For the signs?" Eddie said.

A.J., enjoying the couch, the cool air, said, "They won't fly."

Cotton was genuinely puzzled. He said, "Why not?"

She said, "You don't have time while you're driving. You can't steer and concentrate like that."

"So you stop?" Cotton said.

A.J. said, "Eddie?"

Eddie had no opinion.

"Try this," Cotton said. He unfolded a piece of paper and read, "Bemoaned a layman of Kent—"

A.J. said, "Kent?"

Cotton ignored her. He said, "Bemoaned a layman of Kent, I've given more than I've spent, curtailing my pith . . ."

"No way is that going to fly, Charles," A.J. said.

He said, "It'll stop them in their tracks."

"You'll cause a wreck," A.J. said.

Eddie said, "How does the rest of it go?"

Cotton shrugged and said, "You decide."

Eddie said, "Curtailing his pith? What's pith?"

"Your center," Cotton said. "Your pith is your core. Your essence. Pith makes you what you are."

A.J. said, "And you curtail it?"

"It's a test," Cotton said. "The limerick is a test."

Eddie said, "A test?"

"Sure. Are you worthy of my daughter? What rhymes with 'pith'?"

One Mile Past Dangerous Curve   135

Eddie took the sheet from him. He read it to himself, then out loud. "Bemoaned a layman of Kent, I've given more than I've spent, curtailing my pith . . ." Eddie added, "Drinking fifth after fifth."

Cotton wiggle-waggled his hand. "Make it inspirational," he said. "We're shooting for uplifting."

Eddie said, "Uplifting as in religion?"

"Bent," A.J. said. "It needs to rhyme with 'Kent.' Kent and bent."

"What's supposed to rhyme?" Eddie said.

Cotton said, "It's also a test of whether she's worthy of you."

"Fifth upon fifth," Eddie said. "Only to learn I'm transparent."

Grimaces all around. Silence outside, even from the bullfrogs. Disgust.

Eddie said, "The message is deep. It's about the shallowness of mankind."

"You work on it," Cotton said. "You paint a sign and surprise me. I'll have it put up."

Agreed.

Cotton went into the kitchen and came back with Rolling Rock. He said, "More beer?"

"More beer," Eddie said.

"A.J.?" Cotton said. She reached for the bottle he held out for her. Cotton told Eddie he would find out who Kefauver was. Cotton would see what he could do. "I'm not without methods," he said. "Hold onto your horses before you do anything yourself. Don't shut the barn door. Don't misstep."

A.J. ordered pizza, and she and Eddie drove into town for it.

136   Darrell Spencer

He told her her dad was saying Kefauver and his boys probably were growing marijuana out in the cornfields.

"It happens more than you'd believe," she said.

Eddie said, "The more I think about it, the more I think it was Matthew and Mark in the truck."

Disturbed her. She said, "That's not good."

Eddie said, "Skinheads grow pot?"

"Everybody needs money," she said. "There's as much pot growing in these hills as there is anything else. It's easy to hide it."

"Capitalism at work in the heartland."

"Who knows who does what, Eddie?" A.J. said. "You got two super-smart boys riding around in a pickup and thinking that skinheads are cool."

"Gifted," Eddie said.

"I forgot," she said. "Two gifted boys riding shotgun for the local skinheads."

"Family shit," Eddie said.

She said, "Big time."

"You mean kidnap," Eddie said to Noah.

Noah said, "*Retrieve them* is the language you're supposed to use. Matthew and Mark will be retrieved."

"They're eighteen. They have a right to be on their own."

"They shaved their heads. They got tattoos. They're running around and carrying guns like it's a hundred years ago. Like it's what normal people do."

Eddie had come to letter the wall of Noah's dealership. Later

One Mile Past Dangerous Curve   137

he would be hanging a banner. Next door a Carter Lumber was going up. Big trucks rolled in and out. There was a six-foot chainlink fence around the property.

Noah said, "You know what I've got in boxes at the house? Puppets Matthew made when he was six. They're better than any you've seen in a store. The boys did skits. Mark wrote plays—Angie's got those somewhere—and they'd have us come into their room where they would be all set up, and they would perform a play for us." Noah shook his head like he needed to clear it, as if he had water in both ears. He said, "Once, after dinner one night, they interviewed me like they were newscasters. I don't remember exactly what they said, but they asked me about Palestine and Camp David. They mentioned the president of Russia by name."

There were no cicadas. There was no buzz, no thrumming, no sense that Eddie was in a sci-fi film. Their fling was over. Their going had happened like the flip of a coin. They had gone back underground for seventeen years.

A week ago, Mark and Matthew had shown up at Noah's. Cue-ball heads. Flashing their ink, tattoos on their shoulder blades right where Eddie had seen them. Tattoos on their necks. Dragons there, Olive Root thought. Or maybe Chinese letters. They were wearing no shirts, but army fatigues for pants. Noah was out of town. The boys took off, and Olive Root phoned him. She told Noah his boys looked like plucked chickens. She said Matthew and Mark walked in the front door, and she hightailed it out the back door and ended up near the garden in the side yard. She noticed a pickup across the street.

138   Darrell Spencer

She composed herself behind a short fence. The boys didn't take much. Clothes, she thought. The TV from their room. Mark carried out a duffel bag and one suitcase. Matthew took a couple of deer-hunting rifles.

He was hauling them past her and she dared a couple of steps toward him. She said, "It's good to see you boys are well."

Got in return nothing but swagger.

"You all done?" Olive Root said.

Mark had only a grin for her. A knot where there ought to have been a mouth. Creepy. Apocalyptic.

Matthew, returning, said, "One more look around first." Olive Root didn't budge.

Mark scrambled into the back of the truck, and Matthew went inside. He came out empty-handed. "Ms. Olive Root," he said, "you understand this is nothing against you or Noah. We wish the two of you only the best. You're good people. You might begin to consider advancing the cause yourself."

"The cause?" she said.

He winked. Then he glanced at the truck, which was U-turning, and he said, "You tell Noah we're thinking we're all even at this point."

"For eighteen years?" Olive Root said.

Matthew, on the move, said, "What's that?"

She said, "What about Yale?" She stepped sideways, put a shrub between her and him. There was a concrete squirrel at her feet. By her side, two cement white-tailed deer, tall as she was.

Matthew upgraded from jog to trot—anyone could see he

One Mile Past Dangerous Curve   **139**

would have to hit the truck on the run—and he yelled, as he climbed in, "Not for us." He raised a fist in the air.

So Noah phoned his Las Vegas pal, a guy named Benny, a man whose family was old-time Las Vegas and who Noah grew up with. Benny said not to sweat it. He said, "Man, hang up. I'm on another line dialing a number as we speak."

Noah said, "But—"

Benny said, "Noah, hang up. I'm the answer man. Your fortune cookie says all your troubles have sailed."

"Do—"

"Say good-bye, my friend," Benny said. "And come see me when you're in town. Bring your boys. They'll be with you."

Not quite twenty-four hours later, two men knocked on Noah's front door, dressed like Mormon missionaries from their black suits and skinny ties to their humbler-than-thou fat shoes. These were men, though, not boys, and they were big enough to play hardball on Sundays. They asked for a photo of Mark and Matthew and said they would call. They told Noah they already had leads in their pockets. They refused him their names. The one who looked like Clark Kent said, "When we need to talk, when all of us get together, call me Butch and him Butch too."

There was a joke somewhere in there but Noah wasn't up to it. It was all okay with him.

Clark Kent–Butch said, "This can get messy."

The other Butch nodded and said, "We call, you come, double-time. Shoeless, hatless, shorts inside out—you see what I'm saying? So give us all the numbers where we can reach you."

Butch said, "We do what time and situation call for, and we don't hesitate. Opportunity don't knock twice."

The other Butch said, "The law is not a consideration."

Noah had not called Benny because he wanted legal. He knew what the police could not do.

Butch said, "You tell no one."

Olive Root, under an arched doorway to the kitchen, tick-tocked her lips and threw away the key.

Here with Eddie, Noah was wearing a pager, and he had a cell phone in his shirt pocket.

"It's kidnapping no matter how you explain it," Eddie said. He taped a pattern to the brick wall of the dealership. "Your boys could press charges. Sue you. Have you thrown in jail."

Noah said, "Who's asking for a lecture?"

"You can't force eighteen-year-old legal adults to do any-thing." Eddie rubbed a pounce bag along the letters cut into the pattern. SNAPPER, all caps, three feet high. An hour ago, he finished the pictorial, a mower and Mr. Home Owner running it, his face saying, *Nothing could be easier.* Eddie said, "They don't have to live with you. They don't have to go to Yale."

Noah said, "I'm not stupid."

"I'm just saying."

Noah said, "They're my sons. These kind of people snatch runaways all over the country. They de-something them." He worked the heel of his shoe on pea gravel. Hurtlike. Put upon. How had this happened to him? "My God, what's eighteen?" he said. "What did you know at eighteen?" He was living in a circle of doubt. He said, "Squat is what you knew, Eddie, and squat is what they know."

"I'm not arguing with you," Eddie said.

"Squat," Noah said, "is what I know."

Eddie removed his pattern and rolled it tight. Noah helped him snap top and bottom lines. The color would be Snapper red. Eddie had already painted a banner to drape across the bottom. It said GRAND OPENING and listed some sale prices. Green lettering, a foot high. Eddie wasn't going to let Olive Root rule the world. Not on his life. You might as well turn things over to the late-night psychics.

"They're not bounty hunters," Noah said. "They do this for a living. There are safe places they take kids to."

Eddie unwrapped a brush, dipped it in thinner, wrung the oil to the ground. He shook out a rag and used it to dry the bristles. He poured the Snapper red in a sixteen-ounce cup he had cut down. He stirred the paint and said, "Benny say what they are?"

Noah said, "They retrieve things. That's what he said."

"So they're on the up-and-up in some way? It's a job they do regularly?" Eddie said. "They have badges?"

"They seemed professional. Like they knew what they were doing. Like they did this all the time. You know, health care workers."

Eddie said, "Benny sent you health care workers?"

"Something like that."

"Professionals?"

142   Darrell Spencer

"I'm assuming," Noah said. "If anyone knows what he's doing, it's Benny."

Eddie said, "He's who I'd turn to."

"Which I did," Noah said.

"Are you paying a lot?"

"I didn't ask."

Eddie cut in the outline of the SNAPPER *S*. He said, "They're Benny's guys, then?"

"We're going around and around," Noah said. "You and me, we don't need to go around and around like we're doing."

Eddie said, "You got to worry a little."

"I don't give a real flying fuck who or what they are," Noah said. He wobbled on the gravel, like the sun and humidity had gotten to him. It was all too much. Bad things, crazy things, unbelievable things happening to good people. He dug a Pepsi out of Eddie's cooler. Noah stalled here where he stood. "I had two boys on their way to Yale," Noah said. "A doctor. A lawyer. Whatever it was they were talking about doing. Maybe president of the country. Now——" He couldn't open his drink. He said, "They're trashing their lives. You commit a felony, you don't ever vote. You can't ever vote, no matter what you do. So they wad up their lives and throw them away."

Eddie cut the corner on the first *N* in SNAPPER and set his brush and paint aside. "What can I do?" he said to Noah. He got his own Pepsi. Opened it, handed it to Noah. Then opened Noah's for himself.

"We wait is what the Butches told me."

"They bring them to the house?" Eddie said. "They phone you? What? They call and you come running, like they said?"

Noah shook his head. He said, "They take the boys to a motel room. That's what you see on the news."

Eddie said, "You do?" He located his cup of paint and said, "What then?"

"They call, I come," Noah said. He touched his cell phone. He said, "They think Matthew and Mark have been programmed in some way. Because that's what they said. They deprogram them. That was the word. Deprogram."

"Noah," Eddie said, "I think your boys want to be outlaws for a little while. They want to play with fire. It's part of being as smart as they are."

"The Butches said they'd call. It's all I know."

"Here," Eddie said, and he passed Noah a three-inch brush. It was for poster paint, but would do the job. Eddie poured Noah a cup of Snapper red and said to him, "Follow me and fill in." Noah uselessly rotated the brush he held, and Eddie said, "It will take your mind off waiting on that phone to ring."

Noah wasn't moving.

"Paint," Eddie said. "Paint."

Noah said, "My boys. Olive Root said she was confronting evil itself. What does that mean?"

"She has an overwrought view of things," Eddie said. "Maybe you've noticed."

Noah said, "No argument from me on that." He set the brush on the Toyota's tailgate. He said, "She told me Mark walked and held his fists like he was ready to hit her." Noah cut a glare at the sky. He said, "Olive Root said she didn't want to go in the house after they left. She was thinking they'd planted something. That they booby-trapped it. That's foolish thinking, sure, but that you

144 Darrell Spencer

have to consider the idea, that you even think about—that's sad. Matthew and Mark, they took our rifles. Theirs. Mine."

"Looking a certain way isn't the same as being that way," Eddie said. "Like you were saying, they're eighteen. They're testing themselves, and they're trying stuff out." He finished cutting in the *R*. He said, "Mark and Matthew, they've been good kids a long time. It's part of them." Eddie started filling in letters.

"You're telling me it's a phase?"

"They need to rebel."

"Being a skinhead is a phase?"

"I'm saying it's likely. They're too smart for that shit."

"I mean this isn't like having to wear the right pants. This is more than a fashion statement."

"True. No question it is."

"This could end bad in a thousand ways."

Noah walked out to the berm of the highway and stood there. Traffic flying by. The dealership was too late opening. He had screwed it up. You don't sell mowers after June, into July, come August. First year was going to be a write-off.

Eddie, in his trailer, spread out the cards Patty dealt him all those years ago. One by one by one by one on a TV tray. Left to right, he arranged them in the order she had laid them down. Here they were, fanned out. Seven of diamonds, five of clubs, five of diamonds, four of diamonds. The hand he had been dealt.

Not by some god, but by the woman he loved. What could be better?

You don't get over a lady like Patty.

So smart a woman. Part hood. Part angel.

Seven plus five equals twelve. You're in a bit of trouble. Bad cards. Then add five. Seventeen. Every shark and book on how to play said stand on seventeen. Any nimrod with an IQ above sixty would. Patty was showing the king. Likely, all the math said, she would bust.

Stand pat.

Where was the fun in that?

"Hit," Eddie had said.

"Ah, Eddie," she said. The story of their marriage. *Ah, Eddie. Oh, Eddie.*

Once Patty bailed him out of the drunk tank. She wrangled him into the car, got in, started the engine, looked at him, and said, "Thus, Eddie." Eddie Dancer, the forgone conclusion.

Up had come that four of diamonds. Twenty-one. Fate's hand, Patty said. A winner. Good fortune's handmaiden.

Eddie collected the cards from his tray.

Ohio. Glen. Joy. Noah, and his boys. All the family shit.

It was one A.M.

Charles Cotton. A.J.

Last time they made love, A.J. on top, Eddie still inside her, she leaned over him, and he wrapped his arms clean around her, and he thought, Ollie Ollie Oxen, All in Free.

It was a start. You put one image in front of another one, and yesterday became tomorrow. It was not a matter of trumping one image with another image. There was no doing that.

146   Darrell Spencer

But A.J. Here was a start.

M&M had sent Eddie a map of Athens, included a printout from a website called Haunted Athens. She highlighted in yellow marker local family cemeteries—the five largest in the area, Zion, Simms, Hanning, Higgins, and Cuckler. They formed a pentagram that enclosed the city. Simms, out on Peach Ridge, was the largest. It was also—M&M underlined this—rated one of the spookiest places on earth. There was a hanging tree, grooves in its branches where the ropes had worn off the bark. You never found the tombstones in the same spot twice. Early morning and around midnight, a figure in black hovered above the mist. Those who knew said it was the hanging judge who walked the ridges, a noose hitched over one shoulder. Dead center of the five cemeteries was Wilson Hall on the university's campus. M&M used red ink and traced the pentagram. Her note claimed the ink she used was blood. She wrote, *Scary?*

On the phone, she had said, "Eddie, you're in a safe zone."

He said, "What am I safe from?"

She said, "You tell me."

So this was how Eddie and his kid played. He called earlier tonight and said, "I thought pentagrams were bad news. Aren't we talking about the devil? About vampires? They stand inside one so you can't get at them? Your silver bullets won't work. It's inside, that's where they kill the chickens?"

Maggie said, "Inside is protected ground."

"For vampires," he said. "That's what I'm saying."

"Eddie, Eddie, we're not talking about vampires. Get a grip on your imagination. You tend to run to the morbid. You're safe living inside the pentagram."

One Mile Past Dangerous Curve   **147**

"We're back to square one. What am I safe from?" M&M had *X*'d Glen and Joy's house. It was near the edge of an angle, but inside the pentagram's hexagon center. Haunted Athens, the website, talked about ghosts. There was a tour you could take.

Eddie's thinking was, Who would want to? What's the thrill here?

"You're safe from the devil, for one, Eddie."

"So you're saying the devil's after me?"

"If the devil was, Eddie, if—God forbid"—here his daughter laughed, all this being that funny—"if the devil got you in its sights, you would be safe in the zone."

He said, "What about his helpers?"

She said, "His helpers?"

"Like Santa has helpers."

"But *his*?" Her tone telling Eddie to reload.

"Oh, right. Got it. Daddy's being sexist." He said, "Its?"

"Better, Eddie," M&M said. "But consider the devil might be a woman. There is plenty of precedent for it."

"What would she be after me for?"

"It's what the devil does. The devil collects people, Eddie. Don't you read anything? The devil is the devil because the devil does what the devil does."

"Which is?"

"The devil collects souls."

"What about ghosts?"

"Are you asking if they are male? Female?"

"No. I'm wondering who is protected. Am I protected from ghosts or only from the devil?"

148   Darrell Spencer

"You're protected from everything, Eddie. Goblins. Demons. Poltergeists. Zombies. The restless. You name it. Your backside is covered totally. As long as you stay inside the zone."

"I still think the pentagram itself is bad news."

"Read my lips, Eddie. You're safe." M&M sighed. He remembered her at age seven. Angry. He had denied what to her was clearly a simple request, and she said, "Pay attention. I'm going to stamp my foot. You know what that means." Now, on the phone, she said, "Eddie, you need to rethink the paranormal. It's not all bad. It can be beneficial. Would I mail you bad news?"

Sure, he thought. Not on purpose, you wouldn't. But yes. Bad news is all about point of view. He said, "How can it be beneficial?"

"Spirit guides, for one."

"Like I said, you're talking ghosts."

"Eddie, Eddie," M&M said. "Friendly spirits. Truth speakers."

Eddie said, "I'm buying me a crucifix."

Now, one or so in the A.M., TNT on, Bette Davis outdoing Bette Davis, Eddie touched each card. Seven. Five. Five. Four. Forward, backwards, inside out, they added up to twenty-one.

Patty and Eddie, they got together and the result was Maggie. Was M&M. Quite a product, that child.

Married, Patty and Eddie, they had a routine, Patty saying, "Eddie, how do you know when you're having a bad day?" and he would say, "The dealer's showing a jack, and you've got

One Mile Past Dangerous Curve   **149**

eights you split. You take a six and a seven like bullets, and the hole card is another jack."

"Hey Eddie," she would say—like the two words were really only one word, as in *HeyEddie*—midnight, the two of them passing in the hall, Patty arriving from work, Eddie sleepless. She would say, "How do you know if you're having a bad day?"

He would say, "Busted at twenty-two, ten hands in a row."

"Time to quit after five or six."

"Sure. Hindsight is twenty-twenty."

Say they drove to the lake, going to get some sunshine. "How do you know it's your worst day?" she would say.

"You've done your count. The deck is full of tens. The dealer's showing a five. Gutsy man that you are you split your nines and next thing you know you're sitting high in the saddle with nineteens like four-star cuisine on your plate. Guy to your left, the anchor, last man at the table, hits a twelve and draws a king. *Hits a twelve*. Busts. The dealer's hole is a ten, and he draws a six. You're living your worst day."

"It's your worstest day."

"Hands down. It's your worstest day."

Thus, Eddie.

The point? Eddie was, every time, every day of the month, every season of the year, going to take a hit on seventeen.

Eddie wanted to talk to Patty. Right now. Here in Ohio. Middle of the night. Because Patty was Patty. He corrected himself and put the phone in its cradle. He opened the trailer's door, and the yard lights flicked on. Ten feet away the mother whitetail and her twins froze. Guilty. Stealing hubcaps. Toilet-papering the neighborhood. Marigold breath, if you could get close enough. Stiff-legged, they fled, skirting a juniper hedge. Each of them swift and graceful beyond expectation.

Roscoe was waiting on the redwood table. Eddie had to give the toad credit. Given Roscoe's height and weight, his getting up here on top would equal Eddie leaping to the roof of Glen's house. Eddie showed the toad a cigarette and said, "You mind?" He settled in next to Roscoe, said, "Okay if I smoke?"

The toad didn't budge. Kept his poker face.

Eddie said, "You're looking thinner."

Roscoe was the picture of glum. He held within his toady body the heft and sadness of lead. The back-yard lights winked off. Fireflies lit their own cigs and darted about in the dark. Zippy, they were. They glowed, then flared out. Red and orange scratches in the night air.

"Roscoe," Eddie said. But he had nothing for the toad. He waved his arms, and the lights lit up the yard. "Presto," Eddie said. Roscoe wasn't impressed. Not in the least.

Useless magic was useless magic.

Eddie could not picture how bad this could all end.

The Rolling Rock was cold. Cotton paced in front of one of the signs Eddie had painted, as if he was window shopping, but deadly serious about it. As if buying mattered. He had combed his hair funny, and it was looking like a speedboat and its wake. He eyeballed the sign. CELEBRATE YOURSELF. Simple-as-pie lettering. Black and white so that Eddie had cut the letters in. He had considered a muted, almost unseeable relief shadow, but dropped the plan. Eddie's thinking had been *less is more*. A.J. sat beside Eddie in a butterfly chair. She said, "I miss the cicadas."

To do so hadn't occurred to Eddie.

"They'll be back," she said. "Every seventeen years like clockwork."

"Can you read it?" Cotton said to A.J. He was looking past her, not listening. He said, ""From where you are?"

Puzzled Eddie.

She said, "It's three words. A two-year-old—"

"Sure, sure," he said. "But can you read it?" He stepped away from the sign and squinted at the lettering. Cotton said, "Get up and walk fast like you're driving."

She said, "I could read it in a tornado." A.J. wasn't about to act like she was in a car. She said, "Go get your glasses."

Cotton said, "I think what I'm getting at is, would it catch your eye?"

"Enough to make me pull over," she said.

"Okay, okay," Cotton said.

Eddie had gone out on a limb. Understatement drove him on this one. Simplicity. White lettering. Black background. He sipped at his Rolling Rock, whistled into the bottle.

Cotton stepped to one side, something Moses-like in the way he stood. "You've outdone yourself," Cotton said. "It's art. It'll end up in the Smithsonian."

Eddie got to his feet and accepted Cotton's handshake.

"Next one's a piece of cake," Cotton said. "It's as easy as making a sandwich." Eddie polished off his beer, listening, Cotton saying, "'Just do it' is all. Three words again. Ornate as hell, though. Knock yourself out. 'Be of good cheer' is the subtext. The message is 'Go about your life singing a happy song.'"

"That's plagiarism," A.J. said.

"We'll give credit," Cotton said.

Eddie said, "Who to?"

She said, "Nike."

"Nike?" Cotton said. He looked to Eddie, who shrugged and said, "To God? I bet it's in the Bible to begin with. Nike probably stole it from there. It's originally God's word."

A.J. said, "It's Nike, you dolts. Everyone knows that." She placed her Rolling Rock at her feet and said, "You don't steal from Nike. They'll come after you. They can't let it happen or everyone's going to rip them off."

"They'll never see it," Eddie said.

She said, "They'll see it."

Cotton said, "Nike is everywhere."

"Like God," Eddie said. "Everywhere and nowhere."

Cotton relaxed in the butterfly chair next to A.J. Eddie sat on the porch's steps.

"Kefauver," Cotton said. "It's his real name." Rumor was he sold guns. His front was an antique store run by people in his family. He dealt coke and its cousins. He was from Tennessee or Mississippi and did a couple of years in a penitentiary. There was trouble in a bar, a fight, and he was convicted of manslaughter. None of it fact. Just stories. Cotton said, "You hear about shit like what he did to you but it doesn't happen to your friends."

"Looking back I don't know how I felt," Eddie said.

"Pissed?" Cotton said.

Eddie said, "Baffled. Like you said, like it shouldn't be happening to me, not in the middle of the day in such a pretty place."

Cotton said, "They probably think they're Robin Hood."

A.J. said to Eddie, "Tell him about Noah."

What? Cotton's look said.

So Eddie told Cotton Noah called a friend in Las Vegas who sent two men to collect Mark and Matthew.

Cotton said, "Two guys from Las Vegas?"

"We don't know. Just that Benny sent them."

"Jesus," Cotton said, the word the sound a rusted bent nail makes when you jerk it from a two-by-four. He said, "Like a damn television show. Two guys from Las Vegas. It's kind of funny, and it's kind of stupid. The goons are here."

"Or worse," Eddie said. "It's real."

"Is Kefauver in some kind of group?" A.J. said to Cotton.

Cotton said, "Nazis, you mean?"

She said, "Skinheads."

Eddie said, "Aren't they the same?"

Cotton said, "Kefauver is a son of a bitch on his own is what I'm hearing. He doesn't have to be in a group to be dangerous. Get five or six dimwits together and a few automatic weapons and you have an army on your hands, however inept and worrisome. They hassle you, and it's sort of like using a picture of your cat to scare mice out of the basement."

That stumped Eddie. "How's that?" he said.

Cotton sipped Rolling Rock. You could see he wasn't quite sure himself. He said, "If we put all the rumors aside, I'm guessing you came close to his crop. What he wants is to keep you out of the area is all. His boys get carried away because none of them got beyond the third grade." Cotton studied his bottle. Polished off the beer. He said, "Last winter a high-school kid near Glouster asks to use a phone up one of the hollows. The result is he comes up missing. Police talk to someone who was there, and the man says there was a story going around that the kid was a narc. The family who let him use their phone is claiming they don't know who he called. He phoned and he left. That's all they know. So the snow melts, and hikers find the body. Natural causes is the verdict. He wasn't a narc. He was a kid who needed a ride."

"He could have gotten lost," A.J. said.

Cotton said, "Don't be buying oceanfront property in Montana, my dear."

She said, "Can you find out for sure about this Kefauver?"

"For sure what?"

"Who he is? What he's doing?"

Cotton said, "Why?"

Which was a damn good question.

She said, "I'm thinking about Matthew and Mark. These boys were going to Yale."

"You sure you saw them?" Cotton said to Eddie.

No, Eddie wasn't. The boys he saw made sure he didn't see them clearly. They kept their faces turned away, like they were too cool for all the fuss that was going on. But would Eddie bet on the two being Matthew and Mark? Yes. And Olive Root had seen the tattoos. She saw them hop into a truck. All the pieces seemed to fit.

Cotton studied hard on Eddie, and then he said, "Here's what I heard, Eddie." Cotton opened another beer. He said, "You embarrassed Kefauver and he can't have you doing that."

"No one knows but me and him about the rifle," Eddie said. "He asked if I was bidding, and I let him know I was trying my wings out."

Cotton said, "Him knowing is enough."

"So we're even," Eddie said. "He robbed me."

"You're even on some other planet maybe."

"This is like high school."

"Way worse. Like you said, this is real."

"What should I do?"

"Look over your shoulder."

"You got any idea how I can stop this from compounding?"

"You can't. But I'm thinking he will."

"It's silly," Eddie said.

"Sure," Cotton said, "like most of life."

Why was still the question. What—should Eddie call the cops? Report his shoes stolen? Cry about the sign they ruined? Noah's boys were of age. They wanted to shave their heads and ride point in a pickup, get tattoos, and run with a horse's ass like Kefauver, give up Yale, they had the legal right to.

What—Kefauver wanted a public apology? Was Eddie sup-

156 Darrell Spencer

posed to buy space in the *Messenger*, the *Athens News*? Take out a full-page?

Wasn't going to happen. The guy robbed Eddie and destroyed his sign. Fucker fucked with Eddie's sign. How childish could all of it get?

Cotton said to Eddie, "I don't mean to sound like I don't care."

Eddie gave him a look that said *no problem*. He stood and said, "You really want a sign that says 'Just do it'?"

"Over my protest," A.J. said.

Cotton nodded yes, gave him the go-ahead.

"You'll end up in court," she said.

Cotton said, "Who's going to notice?"

Eddie said, "Give me two days."

Humping over the long driveway to Liar's Corner Road Eddie caught A.J. and Cotton in his side mirror. They had leaned the sign up against the porch and were admiring it.

"I don't ask," Huntington Bark said to Eddie. Huntington had put together the fact that the man he picked up in his cab and drove to the Blue Diamond Inn was Eddie's father, was Glen. The old guy out of his La-Z-Boy and on the move again. "Three, maybe four times now," Huntington said. Eddie and Huntington were at Roy's, doing more sign business. A new motel was going to be built and its owners wanted a billboard. The Paul Bunyan Festival in Nelsonville had contracted for advertising.

About Kefauver, Huntington had heard pretty much what Cotton had found out. Eddie embarrassed the man. The man wasn't going to stand for it. Word was out.

Huntington said, "He won't let it go."

"What," Eddie said, "is he going to call me out? Is he going to embarrass me back?" Shit happens was Eddie's response. Land slides. Maybe he would paint a sign to that effect. Post it in Kefauver's yard. If the man had a yard, owned a house, didn't move nightly from cave to shack to basement.

Huntington said, "All I'm doing is reporting what I was told."

"Does Glen say what he's up to?" Eddie said.

Huntington said, "He's like doomsday there in my backseat."

"Do you wait? Do you take him home?"

"Me or someone else. We don't sit around and run the meter on him."

Eddie needed a Camel. Big signs in Roy's said there was no smoking. Give enough do-gooders three more ounces of power and there would be no smoking anywhere in the U.S. They would mount a posse and hang you for it. He said, "How long is he there?"

"A couple of hours."

"Every week?"

"I took him twice one week."

"Anyone else going in or out?"

Huntington shrugged. He said, "Like I'm telling you, we don't keep the motor running. We got other fares." Their waitress, one of the owner's daughters, refilled their coffees. She had a thing for Huntington. She touched his shoulder and poured.

"Any guesses?" Eddie said.

Huntington said, "I'd think sex."

"He can't."

"Can't what?"

Eddie said, "He's impotent."

Huntington said, "He's old, but old has been known to do the impossible."

"Not him," Eddie said. "Not at this point."

The waitress said, "Trust me on this one, boys, there's ways of working around being dickless."

Huntington said to her, "Dickless?"

"Same thing," she said and wandered off.

Eddie asked Huntington if Glen was alone at the motel when he picked him up. Did Huntington see any women?

"He comes out by himself," Huntington said. "He comes out from where you register, not from one of the rooms."

Not that it needed to make sense to Eddie. *This* followed *that* only in school. More often it was *that* in spite of all *this* could do about it. Illness took hold, and Glen pined after his losses. You're six, you're sixteen, you're twenty-six, you're thirty-six, and your ignorance is what keeps you moving full throttle. You're alive, and you're in jeopardy. Not knowing squat actually being as important to staying alive as the blood in your veins and the heart that pumps it. Eventually all you could do was put that one foot in. Forget shaking it all about. All that bullshit about history holding the key to the future was exactly what it was. Bullshit. How many philosophers had to say that before it registered?

His deals struck with Huntington, Eddie stood outside in the parking lot. Twenty, thirty, forty cars no bigger than refrigerators sat in rows. Their drivers milling around a small parking area, checking out each other's vehicles. Maybe two rail-thin people could have squeezed into one car. No more. A driver. Maybe a passenger. All of the cars were painted one of the primary colors. Their tires belonged on wheelbarrows.

What was that children's song? It's a small world after all? Some such shit.

No cicadas. Not a peep.

Eddie fired up the Toyota, and he sat back confounded. There was that word EAT in Roy's window, lit up in broad daylight. Three feet high. Red neon. What could be simpler?

Right in front of Eddie: philosophy.

Something had gotten the old guy off his butt.

Eddie exited 33 north of Athens, took Columbia Road so he drove past the Blue Diamond Inn, which, of course, wasn't an inn but a row of dirt-ugly one-story rooms strung along the bottom of a wooded ridge where its parking lot collected trash. Pine trees flanked the building. Others backstopped it. Huntington delivered the university kids here when a couple of them had partied themselves into equal stupors and gotten to the

160 Darrell Spencer

point where it looked like sex might just be the ticket. He drove hookers and their johns here. He drove Eddie's father here.

For what?

Two big-ass cars, both discards from the 1960s, old-time gas guzzlers, were parked in front. Each hogged more than one parking slot. Motel doors were open, and a maid pushed a cart along the walkway. Her hair was orange. She puffed at a cigarette, which inspired Eddie to light his own. He turned onto the access road and stopped. He cracked his window. The maid flicked her cigarette into the lot and ducked into a room. Eddie double-checked his mirror and pulled into traffic.

Joy was at the kitchen sink repotting plants. Eddie didn't tell her where Huntington drove Glen. He had no plans to. Glen left her alone a couple of afternoons. God bless. "He squats in there"—she waved toward the step-down room off the kitchen—"those stupid glasses on, like they're going to work. How idiotic can one person be? A pair of plastic glasses is going to give him twenty-twenty eyesight? At two there's a honk and he's out the door."

"You don't ask where to?" Eddie said.

She said, "I asked the first time, and he shut the door in my face."

"He didn't tell you later?"

"I didn't ask again."

"You don't wonder?"

Joy said, "I haven't learned much in life, Eddie, but I have figured out that what you don't do is look a gift horse in the mouth." She held a snapdragon so she could get a good look at the roots against the light, then worked the flower into a terra-cotta pot. Overhead a toilet flushed. They heard Glen move along the hallway. She handed Eddie a couple of plastic pots, collected two herself, and they headed for the patio out back. A door shut upstairs. She said, "Best to stay out of his way." Eddie elbowed the slider open, and Joy, stepping through, said, "He's like a bowling ball loose in the house."

They set the plants on a wrought-iron table, and Eddie said, "It's good he's going places."

"You'd think so," Joy said. She switched flowers around and checked the sky like she had sunlight on a timer.

Eddie said, "It gets him out of your hair?"

"Not really," Joy said. "He's always in the back of my mind."

"But the TV's off? It's quiet for an hour or two?"

"But I'm always listening." She put a hand to her ear. "You know he's not done, so I'm listening."

That was when the phone rang, and the machine picked it up. Olive Root on the other end, incoherent, climbing some wall. She sounded like a dog howling. "Noah," she was saying. "Noah. Joy. Eddie."

Eddie hurried in and picked up.

Olive Root said, "Noah."

"Not here," Eddie said.

"No. No. No," she said.

"What?"

"What? What?" Olive Root said.

Eddie said, "He's not here."

"Now. Now." A dog moaning.

"Is he home?"

"Now he's home," she said. "Now. Now he is." She was weeping. She said, "Eddie, I'm scared to death."

Eddie reached Noah's in fifteen minutes. The long story, as Noah told it, as Olive Root told it, was that last night Noah made a Coca-Cola run to one of the drive-thrus. Olive Root had rented a movie, had it in the VCR, had fast-forwarded through the previews. She was all set up, one finger on the play button, comfy in the scrubbies she slept in and her Happy Feet slippers. The popcorn was air-popped. No butter. One of your heart-conscious treats. It got to be nine-thirty. Okay. No big deal. Ten rolled around. No Noah. The popcorn was cold. Fine. It was cheap. She popped a fresh batch. Would have given him butter this one time if he asked. If, God be blessed, he returned in one piece. Noah must have run into buddies and gone for that one beer he was allowing himself now and then. That was all. No big deal. Eleven rolled around. Now the man was in trouble. "In blame with me," she said to the TV. He would pay. Eleven-thirty. This was annoying. Okay, he stopped for a drink and the NFL was on. She checked the channels. Yup. The Minnesota Vikings and the Chicago Bears. Preseason. Insensitive of Noah, but manly. Twelve o'clock. Stressful didn't cover it. Rude came close. At one A.M. she phoned the sheriff's office, then the highway patrol. She called the Nelsonville hospital and O'Bleness emergency over in Athens. Feeling like a pan-wielding spouse, a schoolmarm, she phoned bars. Outside, she paced the porch. She noticed a truck cruising up and down the street, inches from the curb, its engine running. She called the cops again. Seven A.M. O'Bleness phoned.

The highway patrol had brought Noah to emergency. She was not to worry. He was fine. Likely a fractured arm was all, and he was prepped for stitches.

The good news was the arm wasn't broken, which was the first thing Olive Root told Eddie when he walked in the door. It was battered and sprained and in a sling. Noah dislocated his wrist was all. The doctor put stitches in his forehead. "They did something to the Butches," Noah told Eddie, who had come alone. Joy begged off riding along. "Can't, can't, can't," she said. "No," she said. "Call me and tell me what's going on." She said, "Enough is enough. Enough's more than enough."

Noah filled Eddie in. He tipped back into his La-Z-Boy, pillows fluffed up around him, and he said, "They left me the Butches' driver's licenses." Their names were Jackson and Lawrence Smith. From Cleveland, not Las Vegas. Noah talked and sipped the tea Olive Root kept delivering.

Whoever they were who had done something to the Butches, *they* abducted Noah. He was driving his old banger Oldsmobile, the car he kept for work. He pulled into the drive-thru, ordered two cases of Budweiser, a bag of Doritos corn chips and salsa, asked about a Paul Bunyan Days t-shirt Olive Root was wanting, then leaned sideways in the seat to fetch his wallet from his back pocket, and his door and the passenger door were jerked open. Two seconds and the passenger's side was full of a dude big as a tank. Men climbed in the back, and the guy who had opened Noah's door shouldered Noah into the middle. And just like that Noah had a ski mask over his head. The little he had seen and felt— a whack to the side of his head, a forearm to his ribs—had him thinking he had been thrown into a football game at the line of scrimmage. If there were eyeholes in the mask, they were turned so Noah couldn't use them. He sat wedged between two guys twice his size. At least two more in the backseat. Maybe three. No one said a word. They drove for what seemed like hours and could have traveled two hundred miles or the same five miles over and over given the way the roads all returned on themselves. One instant before the men climbed in his car, Noah noticed that it was that time of night when the sun's gone down and the sidewalks and driveways absorb the afterglow. The pavement was white, flat.

Noah begged them to take the car and let him go. He said, "I've got a wife, kids." He pleaded—Whatever you want. Don't hurt me. Whatever you want—and he offered them the sixty he had in his wallet. He said he would hit an ATM if they wanted. He had three thousand in his account and could get another five grand if they let him make a call. What he got back was the stink of men who didn't shower. Noah tugged at the mask where his mouth was, and the guy in the passenger's seat smacked his hand. Like Noah was a bad boy sucking his thumb. It was a cave in the car. Fucking cave and cavemen sitting out the night. Waiting for the sun god to get his ass out of bed. Squat in the cave. Take his morning dump in the sand. Grunt. Get the day on its feet.

Someone in the backseat lit up. A cigar. Civilization.

Noah picked at the mask and said, "Smoke?"

Caveman to his right fiddled in his own pocket, tapped free what turned out to be a cigarette, and lit it. Blew smoke Noah's way. He said, "You like that?"

Noah said, "How about it? Spare one?"

The man shifted in his seat, and Noah heard a knife click open. Caveman pinched the ski mask away from Noah's face, hacked a hole in it, and poked in the cigarette. He said, "I don't want you using your hands. Don't raise your hands."

"God bless you," Noah said, the talking almost costing him the smoke. The cigarette wobbled on his lips. He took a drag, and the man removed it and said, "That'll have to do. I'm not the baby-sitter."

"One more," Noah said. "Just one more."

The man obliged him.

Rain was falling. "Wipers?" the driver said. "How do I turn them on?"

Noah reached over. Again with the smack. "Jesus," Noah said.

"Tell me where the switch is," the guy said.

Noah couldn't. Tried to picture the steering wheel, the lights, the lighter, the wipers knob. No dice. He said, "God's sake, I can't do anything to you. Let me feel for it. Like I'm at the wheel."

"You try something, and I'll crack your head wide open," the driver said.

Noah said, "Fair warning." He found the switch and flicked the wipers to high.

"Here she comes," Caveman said. "Get the rowboats ready."

The rain thickened, and the driver braked. Rain so hard it was like a crowd had circled the car and was pounding, two-fisted, on the hood, the cab, the trunk. Persistent. Urgent. Like this was a riot. The driver backed up and onto the shoulder. He

166   Darrell Spencer

must have stopped under a tree, the car on an upslope. The banging rain eased. Then came harder. A big wind was blowing, rocking the car. A tree limb cracked. Then there was lightning Noah could see through the mask. Thunder like cannon fire.

"Judas Priest," one of the men in the backseat said.

Noah had been through these Ohio thunderstorms. You couldn't call it a rain. Water gushed from thick clouds and was whirlpooled by the wind. It flushed the earth. He stood in his house one morning, one foot from a bay window, Olive Root saying, "Get away from the glass." She took his arm. He didn't budge. "Don't use the phone," she said. "Shut off the computer." Noah felt like he was on a tugboat at sea. Olive Root wandered from room to room. "No basement," she said. "You don't live in a house in the Midwest without a basement." But that was exactly what they were doing. Noah said to her, "You're thinking of a tornado."

She ended up sitting in the empty bathtub singing Beatles songs.

Now, another flash, then thunder rolling. There was a noise Noah swore to Eddie was a blowtorch being lit.

Next, hail, which sounded like tacks being tossed at the windshield.

One of the men in the backseat said, "This is what it means to be in the red. You know what I'm saying? On those radar maps? The weather reports on the TV? Light blue is rain. The lighter the rain the lighter the blue."

"That's vertigo you're talking about," the driver said. "Blue is temperature."

"Say what?" the one in the back said.

The guy in the passenger's seat said, "Vertigo means the rain don't reach the ground. That's how shit-ass weak the light blue is."

Driver said, "Blue is temperature, I'm telling you."

"Green is vertigo," somebody said.

"You say so," the man who opened this conversation said. "You hold your opinion. I hold mine. Truth will come out. Right this minute my point is what's on us is the red. The yellow is bad news. The red is get the fuck out if you can."

"We ain't red yet."

"Fuck we're not."

"Five bucks says we're under red."

"You're covered."

A guy from the backseat said, "How will you know?"

"I'm taping," the driver said.

"You're taping the news?"

"I'm taping the news. I tape everything."

"Christ. The news is on all night."

"Not the weather. They don't repeat the weather. It's updated. Always updated. They're not going to go back and show what rain was on us. They move ahead."

"Jesus, man, there's a weather station. All they do is weather. All day long and all night long."

The caveman in the passenger's seat told them both to shut up.

"I'm only pointing out—" This from the man who had started the weather talk, and Caveman sitting next to Noah almost took Noah's head off turning to shut the guy up.

There was a flash of lightning and in a minute the tick-tick of hail. The driver said, "The hair on my arms is curling."

"We're about to get it, then."

"You see to drive?" Caveman said.

"It's almost gone," the driver said. "We're staying put."

The weather guy said, "Hair on——" He clammed up.

Then it was quiet, like a curtain had been pulled, the play was over. The hail quit. The rain slowed. There was no wind left. Noah could hear water dripping.

One of the guys in the back said, "Row row row your boat."

"Judas Priest," the driver said.

Somebody said, "Come hell or high water."

Caveman joined in. "Row row row your boat."

One by one they all jumped on the song. *Row row row your boat, gently down the stream.*

"Fucking singing men of Ohio," the driver said. He pulled onto the road.

The highway patrol found Noah five minutes outside of Chauncey. At one point, about half an hour after the storm quit, Noah felt the car slow, turn right up a knoll, and bump onto railroad tracks. The driver stopped it right on top, or so Noah imagined. The men in the back bailed, one of them touching Noah's shoulder and saying in a whisper that plunged Noah into despair, "Best of luck to you."

The driver climbed out, told Noah to turn so his back was to him, and he handcuffed Noah, hands behind. Uncomfortable as hell. Noah couldn't sit up straight, had to lean left or right. A truck drove off. Another vehicle—truck? van?—idled nearby.

The driver spun Noah in the seat and got back in. Caveman

in the passenger seat—this guy had to weigh three hundred pounds—he put what felt like a baseball card into Noah's shirt pocket, one, and a second one, and he said, "My brother lives in another state, long ways away from here, one a your flat states where they're very serious about the corn they grow, and he's got himself a seventeen-year-old daughter who is beginning to believe she is the queen of these United States, and he has a wife who gets herself dressed about four in the afternoon. Her idea of cooking is a phone call to KFC. Delivery, not pick-up. She claims she has a disease that means she needs to stay calm and sit a lot. My brother, who, by the way, is a police officer, he finds his daughter's diary, and it's full of talk about sex. About how she likes to suck cock. How she likes boys to come on her." This Bubba sounded to Noah like a weed whacker, at half throttle, real low, garbled. He said, "She's written down words my brother—and we're talking about a man who's heard a lot, even though his town is a small one—my brother, he had to go to a dictionary for. He wrote the words out on a piece of paper and took it to the local library in town. *Fellatio. Cunnilingus.* The lady who runs the library guides him over to an unabridged dictionary. Something told him not to show her the words. Which turned out right for him not to do. You didn't move the book from where it was on a podium. You stood and studied it that way. My brother, he writes out the definitions, and he folds up his paper and puts it in his wallet."

The driver lit a cigarette and stuck it in Noah's mouth. He told Noah to stop squirming. To quit bumping him. "Careful of the ash," he said. "We don't want no accidents here."

170 Darrell Spencer

"Fire is one of your big-time worries," Caveman Bubba said, and—no other word for it—the man giggled. Three hundred pounds, and he was squeaking like a girl. He said, "My brother, he asks his daughter one night does she want to go to the DQ, and she's pouty for no clear reason on God's green earth, but goes along, so he drives her out of town, her saying, 'Where we going? I got a date. Bobby's coming over.' My brother tells me her face is all red and crushed-looking so it's all he can do to keep from reaching one hand over and choking her."

Ash dropped to Noah's crotch, and the driver said, "Ah, shit."

"Got us that fire, maybe," Caveman Bubba said.

Noah was helpless. He scooted and twisted. He wasn't getting burned, but could see himself going up in flames and these two hauling ass in different directions.

The driver said, "It's out, folks. Move it along. Nothing more to see here." He snatched the cigarette from Noah's mouth and said, "Resale of this vehicle ain't what it was five minutes ago. Got yourself a nasty burn on the seat."

Noah still worrying over his privates.

Caveman Bubba said, "So my brother drives his daughter out to where there are some railroad tracks, and he parks so they're sitting right where the train is going to come barreling through."

"Like we done this minute," the driver said.

Noah said, "You done what?"

"Like where we're parked this minute."

One Mile Past Dangerous Curve   171

"My brother says to her *trust*," Caveman Bubba said. "I tell you he's a cop? I did. He handcuffs his daughter to him, which is where we got the idea from for you. He handcuffs her to his wrist and he says to her, 'Trust is all we got.'" Bubba told Noah that his brother's daughter was freaking out because where they were the land was flat as a tabletop and she could see the railroad tracks coming at her. Bubba said, "Trains was always passing through. Wait ten minutes and you'd see one." What his brother told his daughter was that he was going to look out his window and she was going to look out hers, and they were going to trust each other to see the trains coming. They would be each other's lookout. "My brother's daughter screams at him," Caveman Bubba said. "She yells, 'This is stupid.' She says, 'It don't even make sense.' And my brother, he said, 'It don't have to. I'm your father.'"

"You get it?" the driver said to Noah.

Noah said, "You're my lookouts?"

"He don't get it," the driver said.

Caveman Bubba said, "He doesn't have to."

Noah said, "I'm supposed to trust you?"

The driver said, "We're leaving. You got no lookouts." He patted Noah's pocket where it would turn out he had put the driver's licenses of the two Butches. "Trust ain't our point."

"I don't get it," Noah said.

Caveman Bubba said, "My brother's daughter eventually did."

"You're saying I will?" Noah said.

The driver said, "Not saying anything of the kind. Be quiet, now. We need to relax and listen."

For a long time there was just their breathing and the other vehicle idling outside. The driver lit another cigarette and said, "You hear about those truckers driving into Washington, all pissed off about the price they're paying for gas?"

Noah said, "Me?"

"You see anyone else around?" the driver said. He buzzed his window down.

"Him?" Noah said, nodding toward Caveman Bubba.

Caveman Bubba said, "They're idiots." Idiots came out ee-diots.

"Ain't they," the driver said.

Caveman Bubba said, "They haul their frigging asses in there—two hundred, three hundred semis, right up the main roads so they slow a few people down, a bunch of dickheads thinking they're causing real hard-ass trouble, and some politician meets them on the steps of some freaking monument, promises them things are going to change, and the newspapers show up. It's a photo op is all it is."

"People blowing smoke up each other's ass."

"Mutual smoke blowing."

"Goddamn photo op."

A train whistle rose from the south. Far away. Could have been on any track in the state.

"Ee-diots," Caveman Bubba said.

"They want to get results," the driver said, "what they do is they block off the freeways. They surround D.C. and shut down the U.S. transportation system. They don't let anybody in, and they let no one out. They hold those senators and congressmen hostage."

Caveman Bubba said, "Ee-diots."

"You want a last drag?" the driver said to Noah.

Noah shook his head no. There was another train whistle. This one closer and, Noah was willing to bet, moving along the track his car rested on.

"There's our wake-up call," the driver said, and he was out the door. Caveman Bubba was gone. "I'd say you got ten minutes," the driver said, leaning in the open window. He said, "They tend to run late here." Noah heard what sounded like a three-hundred-pound-and-growing Caveman Bubba climbing into the bed of a truck, and the driver said to Noah, "I'm betting on you. Doors are unlocked. Car's in neutral but the brake's set. Best of luck." The man was gone. Then back, saying, "Oh, don't waste time looking for these," and Noah heard keys jangling. Then he heard them sailing through the air and the sound of them hitting foliage. The man said, "You won't be needing them."

Noah wiggled and squirmed toward the door, trying to work the mask off, rubbing it against the seat. He succeeded only in screwing it up so the mouth hole they cut ended up around his ear. He scooted to the door and got it opened, but fell out, reacting quickly enough to spin and hit first his shoulder, then his arm on the tracks. He lay there, then heard the whistle. He scrambled to stand and banged his head on the open door. Cut it bad, clean through the mask. He sensed that immediately. Blood was running down his face. He was woozy. He felt the vibration of the train in the tracks. One was coming, was not far off—he could see its lights through the ski mask—and Noah crawled behind his car, put his back to it, dug his feet in, and pushed. He lowered his shoulder, barely managing to rock the car back and forward. The brake. He hurried around the car and released it. The train got louder, and Noah shoved the car a foot, then jumped aside and it caught the hill. The car rolled past him backwards, picked up speed, and Noah stumbled after it. He stubbed his toe on what must have been track and went down, twirling like a drunk, staggering to right himself, crossing through gravel and high grass. He rolled his ankle—pain like someone whacked it with a baseball bat—and he went down. His head hit a fence post. Same spot as before. More hurt to make him die. The mask was knocked off. The car crashed through brush, crossed a highway, shot left and stopped.

Noah was sitting on gravel and dirt, resting against the fence post his head had banged into, when the train passed. It couldn't have been more than thirty feet away. But it was on another track. They had parked him on a side spur that hadn't seen a train in twenty years. Noah's forehead was bleeding, bad, blood coating one side of his face. He tried stepping through his handcuffed hands, but that was a pipe dream, that was a trick for a fifteen-year-old eighty-pound kid.

He got up and walked. Fell. Stood. Fell. He kept hitting his knees. He rolled, one time, down an embankment, lay in mud and water and weeds. He followed the tracks into town, where he sat on railroad ties in someone's front yard. Light soaked up the night, and he discovered he was sitting on some kind of shrine. Three tiers of it, patches of tilled dirt boxed in by the railroad ties. Foregrounded in the first section were lawn-art critters and a birdbath. Rabbits, squirrels, chipmunks, skunk, a raccoon. Next tier up was a fox, orange as a pumpkin. It had black ears and black forelegs in the front. Then, highest tier, there stood a plaster Jesus in a blue robe, Jesus in an alcove, Jesus holding an eagle ready for flight.

It took Noah an hour to convince the highway patrol he hadn't been out drinking with buddies, that what happened was not a prank. He told them to check the video at the drive-thru. They'd see.

Eddie asked Noah if he was going to call Benny.

"And say what?" Noah said. "That his guys are dead?"

"Who says they're dead? They're not dead. You don't kill people that easily in real life."

Olive Root said, "More tea?"

Eddie said, "Their driver's licenses could mean anything."

Noah held his cup so Olive Root could reach it, and she poured tea. He said, "Yeah, like they're dead."

"Farfetched," Olive Root said.

Eddie said, "You still have to call Benny."

"You weren't there," Noah said, and he sank deeper into his pillows.

Eddie said, "What does that mean?"

Noah said, "They didn't care if I got out alive or dead."

Eddie said, "The track wasn't in use."

"I didn't know that."

"They were playing with you," Eddie said. "That tells me they didn't do anything to Benny's guys."

"Not really," Noah said. He rubbed his bandaged arm and

176   Darrell Spencer

said, "I was in handcuffs. Do you see what I mean? They wished me good luck. What does that say about them?"

The Blue Diamond Inn had burned. Not quite to the ground, but most of its long roof had collapsed. Had there been a war on you would have said bombed. The single-file motel was toast. Cops were rerouting cars rolling into town, and fire engines blocked the access road. There was a paramedic rig, the highway patrol, city cops—conflagration and its aftermath. Soot and ash and cinder and firefighters flat-footed, their heads in their hands. White-blue smoke floated among pine trees. The fire was smoldering. A crew crab-walked along the parking lot, soaking hot spots. Traffic backtracked to I-33 and rolled into town at East State.

Eddie was into a U-turn, and A.J. said, "There's Glen." Eddie pulled onto the berm.

Glen stood with a group a policeman was talking to. As if they were at a party, a mixer. All of them waiting on appetizers. Glen, a Coke in hand, pointed at the fire. Next to him was a tall brunette who had arrived on a time machine out of Victorian England. She wore layers of heavy clothes, and only a corset could account for her waist. She had to be wearing a hoopskirt. Her shoes were the old-fashioned pointy high-ankled kind, the ones you laced using a hook. At her elbow, unglued in stance and face, vibrated a jockey-sized remnant from the sixties, a five-foot-one buckaroo who was most likely radical in his heyday, a guy in a black t-shirt, *Rolling Stones* big lips on the chest of it, black Levi's, snub-nosed silver-buckled harness boots. A gray-and-black ponytail rode his spine. Bet him a thousand dollars he couldn't hold still for two minutes, and the man would lose every time. He suffered from the harebrained jitters. There were two prototype housewives, Teflon slacks and blouses, ladies who belonged under a hair dryer writing notes to each other. They kept looking around. They were unnerved, like they had detoured into the bad part of a big city and the bus wasn't getting here fast enough. A dude in a three-piece suit seemed to be in charge. He held himself like duty on command.

A highway patrolman stopped Eddie from crossing the barricades troopers had put up.

"My father's over there," Eddie said.

"They're needing to debrief him," the patrolman said.

"Debrief him?"

"Find out what he knows."

As if Eddie wasn't up to the man's jargon. Wasn't part of the twentieth century yet. Eddie said, "He's ill."

"Paramedics examined everyone," the patrolman said. "We need to talk to all the motel guests."

"He was a motel guest?"

"He was here."

"You think he's involved?"

The patrolman said, "Everybody was in one room. They were the only occupants."

"Did someone start the fire?"

The highway patrolman wasn't saying. The man was too

busy being a cop. He had a belt to hitch up. A stance to take here in Athens, Ohio. Eddie yelled Glen's name, and the old guy ignored him. He was telling his tale and had set his shoulders how a host would. Glen zipped his jumpsuit to his throat. He kept talking.

"Can I speak to him for a second?" Eddie said to the patrolman, and he asked Eddie to hold on. He would let Glen know Eddie was here. A.J., who had been waiting by the car, came up. "What's he doing with those people?" she said.

Eddie told her what Huntington had told him about the high schoolers and college kids coming here for sex. About the hookers who booked rooms. "Those ladies are prostitutes?" A.J. said.

Was a mystery to Eddie. Such a conclusion accounted for the Victorian lady and her costume, and it could be stretched to explain the housewives. Someone's fantasy. Formica. Pots and pans. Sex in the kitchen on a country-style table.

Glen acknowledged Eddie, excused himself and came their way, vigor in his step, death, for an afternoon, wadded into a tight package, sealed, and stuffed in his jumpsuit's pocket. Glen saluted the cop, dropped his Coke can in a plastic bag, and cut through the barricades. He was hopped up. Jazzed. Ready to fly into a speech. He rocked on his feet, side to side, like a jock. His face was flushed. He said to Eddie and A.J., "Let's go for a ride."

"Can you leave?"

"Why not? Who's watching?"

"Who are your pals?" Eddie said.

One Mile Past Dangerous Curve 179

Glen said, "Come on," and he beat it for Eddie's truck.

A.J. looped her arm through Eddie's and said, "Let's go. This is going to be interesting or—"

"Crazy," Eddie said. "Or both."

The Victorian lady hollered after Glen. She held up a finger, asking him to wait a minute. She turned to finish what she had to say to the dude in the ponytail.

Eddie, A.J. and Glen waited by the truck, Glen explaining what was going on. It turned out Glen had joined a group of UFO chasers. The core of them ufologists. They met once or twice a week to catch up on the latest visitations. The motel manager—a drifter out of Wyoming—was one. He let them use what had once been a conference room at the Blue Diamond Inn. The fire started in his office at the other end of the motel. The on-the-scene thinking was it was electrical and for unspecified reasons the Wyoming fellow was in deep-shit trouble. Most of the UFO chasers were abductees, one a college student from Peru, one the psychologist who had organized the group. He held a Ph.D. from Harvard and taught at Princeton for fifty-five years. Then he retired to Athens, his hometown. He was your silver-haired gent in the three-piece. He was, he claimed, sitting in the seat next to Ronald Reagan that night over Bakersfield, California, when then–Governor Reagan spotted a UFO out the window of the Cessna he was flying in. The professor didn't want his name bandied about, so he asked the others to call him Leonard Bones. The sixties holdover was seven years old the first time visitors hauled him aboard. He lived in Fargo, North Dakota, back then. He went missing three days and two nights and came to lying in his own front yard. It was pitch-black, and he had no memory of where he had been. The family doctor located a scar on his neck the doctor didn't think he had seen before. His medical records didn't show one. Six years later the same aliens abducted him again. He was thinking they removed whatever it was they had implanted. His neck was tender, and the scar scabbed. Since then, every six years they came, and he lost three days. He always sensed it when they were circling, if circling was what they did. They had an eye on him. He felt that. He was sure they made him have sex at least one time. Yearly, he marked his calendar. Weeks before they snagged him, his nose bled at night, and he fought a headache mean enough to knock him to the ground. He grew older, he married, but refused to have kids, given the circumstances of his life, was divorced and moved to the East Coast. He changed his name, they found him. Their ship was always the same one. It was pancake shaped. He would smell sulfur, and the next thing he knew it would be three days later.

Glen unfolded a map of Ohio and showed it to Eddie. X's dotted it. The map reminded Eddie of the one M&M had sent, but there was no pentagram outlined here, no cemeteries marked. The Victorian woman—her name was Jennifer Evers—had, last night, been privileged to see one of the most common mother ships. Oval, the football shape. A mother ship meant there would be others, soon. Probably tonight.

She finished with the ponytail dude and came over to the truck. She wanted Glen to have her notes. She handed him a sketch which showed the ship's color. She said it was royal blue like a king's robe. She described how the ship moved, how it

One Mile Past Dangerous Curve   181

had vibrated where it hovered. It put out music, organ-like, but not churchy. The craft floated above the trees, and the ground was shaking like she was in an earthquake, a phenomenon she was expert in, her home state being California. Then the ship shuddered and was gone. This was two A.M. She checked the time. She had gone for a ride in her car. Was, she confessed, a restless soul. She felt compelled to pull off the road short of a covered bridge out near Coolville, and there the ship was. The mother ship.

"It's not far from here," Glen said to Eddie, and he opened the truck door. He said, "Let's go."

Eddie said, "You were in a fire? You okay?"

Glen did a jumping jack. "Fitter than a fiddle," he said. "Come on. It's time to live in a hurry."

"What about your leg?" Eddie said.

Glen said, "Get in."

"I'm not saying you'll find any evidence," Jennifer Evers said.

"You never do," Glen said. "But that's not the point, is it? You coming? You can guide us."

"You'll find it," Jennifer said. "I got family to see to. You know, it's impossible for them to feed themselves. Later, we're going to the quilt show, my sister and me."

Eddie said to Glen, "What is the point?"

Glen said, "What do you need to live—a printed invitation?"

Jenny pecked the old guy on the cheek. She had to go. She would call about a new place where they could meet. Maybe her house. Her husband and kids were already thinking she was one foot over the line and so far off the mark there was no coming back for her. She overheard the word *nutcase* more often these days. Why not go whole hog? Give her husband reason to complain. She would have the Twilight-Zone folk over for cake and ice cream and UFO talk.

Glen said to A.J., "I can see you're ready."

"You want to go?" Eddie said to her.

Glen said, "She wants to come. Who wouldn't?"

A.J. did. Eddie checked the traffic and slowed for one last look at the Blue Diamond Inn. Rubble and black-and-whitened timber, end to end, like pick-up sticks. Not a room left standing. Here and there the ragged stack of a brick wall. Firemen looped hoses to hoses, racked them, and city cops herded rubberneckers by. The boxy paramedic truck rolled out and turned toward the freeway. Nothing more to see here. Eddie, A.J. and Glen dipped into town to pick up Glen's binoculars. Joy, outside the house, was thinning her zinnias, the flowers too high and too dry. Birds had begun to eat the seeds she planned to store. Joy was wearing a dress, was standing like a paper cutout.

Glen rolled down the Toyota's window, and Eddie volunteered to go inside for the binoculars. Behind him Glen, loud—the man had no other way—said to Joy, "Grab your coat, honey. Let's take a ride. We can cram ourselves in here."

"Busy, Glen," she said. "You can see I'm busy here."

"Got a date? A gentleman caller?"

She said, "It's only an expression."

"What is?"

She drifted farther away. Posted herself to the ground.

"Gentleman caller?" Glen said.

One Mile Past Dangerous Curve   183

Eddie hesitated at the front door, thought about going back and smacking the old jackass. Maybe put an end to this trip.

Joy was walking toward the truck when Eddie returned. She said to him, "Where to?"

"A UFO sighting," Eddie said. He told her about the fire, the meeting, how this was the answer to where Glen went afternoons. Glen and his ilk. Eddie asked her if she wanted to tag along.

No. Not a chance. Not happening. She came to a halt. She was not going to take one more step.

"It's a drive, is all it is," Eddie said. "Come on. We'll take your car so there's room." He scrutinized her. Thought he saw hope. He said, "He's feeling lively. There's a spark in his eyes."

Nope. Joy wasn't going to feed into it.

"Grab your handbag," Glen said to her from the truck. "Your kit and your caboodle."

She stepped closer to him and said, "You horse's rear end."

Didn't faze Glen. "Get in," he said to Eddie. "Either that, or I'm driving." He said to Joy, "Tell your boyfriend your husband is old and minus his equipment but he can load a pistol and he aims straight. You tell him—"

"You're too much," she said. "You're a nightmare."

Glen said, "Don't you wish."

Joy retreated, was halfway up the walk to the house, Eddie following her, when she stopped and said to him, "He will torture me to my grave. Then he'll climb in and torture me in my grave." She shooed Eddie back to the truck. "You baby-sit him," she said. "Please. Get him out of my hair for an hour. For

184   Darrell Spencer

all I care, you can drop him off in the woods and drive away fast."

At the far end of East State, they bumped into traffic. Five, six light changes to get through an intersection. Cars unable to exit the mall or Kroger's. More of them clogging the side streets. A standstill. Rap thumped from the El Camino in front of Eddie's truck, the car's bed full of mattresses. It was Sunday, which meant no farmer's market. There was no reason for the congestion. Eddie let the engine lug the Toyota along. A.J. sat between him and Glen, no one talking. Low seventies, and they rolled the windows down. Glen folded his map, stuck it in his jumpsuit pocket, and said, "You got a hundred rabbits standing in a row. What do you call it if they all take a step backwards?"

Eddie gave him a look.

A.J. said, "A receding hareline."

"Bingo," Glen said.

Big Bear grocery store was the hang-up. A sale Eddie had painted signs for. FOR THE FRESHEST FOOD AND BEAR MINIMUM PRICES IT'S GOT TO BE THE BEAR. The grocery store had remodeled itself inside out. For today, its parking lot was set up like a county fair. There were kids and balloons. Booths. Rides. There was a big yellow truck, *Dowling Circus, Inc.* on the side. *Chip the Bear,* it said.

"Pull in," Glen said. "Park. Find a spot."

It was a carnival. There was a Dunk the Scouts booth. People were throwing darts and shooting air guns. They were lined up for the funhouse. There was a stage, and there were fiddlers. Eddie circled through once, stop-and-go traffic, and there was

Chip the Bear in a rink. Cool Zone fans sprayed a mist toward the animal. A woman was tossing Frisbees at Chip. She threw, and the bear snatched them out of the air and dropped them into a garbage can. Was expert at it, the woman hurling them one after another. She wasn't bad herself.

Lucky day for the grocery store. The sky clear, perfect weather after three days of drought-ending rain. The woman stopped hurling the Frisbees, and a handler gave the bear a Coke. Chip guzzled it. Trashed the can. Then reset for catching. Chip was loving the spotlight. The bear moved like a tennis pro.

"I pinned me a bear," Glen said.

Eddie pulled ahead, cars behind him, at his doors, inching forward, hemming the truck in. A woman honked.

Glen said, "Park, Eddie." He rattled his doorknob. He said, "Shit. Locked."

"Hold on," Eddie said.

They ended up a quarter of a mile away. Glen hooked his arm in A.J.'s and hurried her toward the rink. Eddie fell in beside them. "I wrestled a bear," Glen said. "I pinned it. I would have won a car but they refused to give it to me." Late 1950s it had been. Joy could vouch for Glen. No. Not Joy. His first wife. Margaret, the one who died thanks to canning fruit and a virus medicine at the time detected too late.

A carnival brought a bear to Las Vegas. Its winter circuit. They set up at Cashman Field. The knucklehead who ran the thing said Glen didn't touch both of the bear's shoulders to the ground simultaneously. They had to be touching at the same time. You pinned the bear you won a Cadillac. The man claimed he saw daylight. He pinched his thumb and finger together, then separated them. "He wasn't all the way down," he said. "There was a good half an inch showing under that right shoulder." The chiseler wasn't giving the Cadillac away. Not on his life. Did so, he lost his job. He could kiss his paycheck so-long. He showed how he ran his hand clean under the shoulder. Glen paid and tried again. Failed. He was worn out. He came back the next night, and he brought friends along. His buddies. He wanted witnesses. Margaret was with him, but the son of a bitch who ran the show refused to let Glen wrestle. He said there was a rule against doing it three times. He pointed out a sign that said he could deny a chance to anyone he chose to deny. If he didn't want you to wrestle his bear he didn't have to let you. He accused Glen of carrying a weapon, of being up to some trick. One of Glen's pals buttonholed teenagers and drunks walking by until he had collected a rowdy crowd. So the guy let Glen wrestle the bear or there was going to be a riot. Glen pinned the bear, faster this time, and the SOB shook his head. He said, "That left shoulder wasn't down all the way." It was a lie. Boldfaced. The crowd got mean. Booed. Hurled beer cans. A kid threw a corn dog, and the bear went for it. So the four-flusher gave Glen fifty bucks and told him to beat it. Which was okay with Glen, fifty dollars being more than a week's pay back then. It was a house payment. He gave forty to Margaret and invited everyone downtown to Fremont Street for a drink.

Glen's leg hurt, he said, felt like it was in a vise, and by the time they got to the rink he was hobbling like he had a flat. "That bear wrestle?" he said to a handler, who ignored the old man. A.J. slipped free of Glen's arm, box-stepped around him, and Eddie moved in next to his dad. Glen said to him, "What do you think they'd pay me to wrestle the bear?"

"You don't need to be wrestling a bear," Eddie said.

Glen said, "What's the bear here for then?"

Eddie said, "The store. It's a theme. It's Big Bear grocery stores."

"Hey," Glen said to the handler, who said, "Pipe down."

"How much you pay me to wrestle your bear?" Glen said. He pushed between two of the thigh-high chainlink sections of fence and limped toward the bear. He was dragging his leg. The woman tossing the Frisbees hesitated mid-throw and sailed one at Chip's feet. The bear stumbled. Got clearly pissed. A second handler rushed at Glen, and another one, near the truck, jogged toward Chip. "I'll take on the bear," Glen said. "There's a crowd-getter for you. Gramps and the bear."

Eddie, a step slow, said, "Glen, let's go."

"Paint a sign for these folks to see," Glen said to him. He talked one into being right there in the parking lot. He said, "*Come See the Amazing Old Coot Pin Chip the Bear.*"

Eddie said, "Dad."

"My boy paints signs," Glen said.

A handler was waving for help.

"It's showtime," Glen said. He tried to get around the second handler, and the man cut him off. "You can do it," Glen said. "Grease me up. I've done this before and won myself a Cadillac. I'm offering you a showstopper for free. Your chance to give these folks a story to tell the relatives in Des Moines.

188   Darrell Spencer

Hey, they saw an old son of a bitch take on a bear and pin it to the ground."

The handler spoke to Eddie. He said, "Can you get him out of here?"

Eddie said, "Dad, let's go." He touched Glen, and Glen jerked away. "You're not in charge of me," he said.

A.J. said, "Glen."

"What, am I too old?" Glen said. "Am I hearing that I'm too old? The old guy can't wrestle the bear."

The handler looked to Eddie.

Eddie said, "Glen, we need to get going." He was about to mention the UFOs, Coolville, the sighting, the covered bridge. Didn't Glen owe his pals? But why compound the insanity.

The handler said to Glen, "Would you like to toss some Frisbees? Some rings?"

"Like I'm two years old," Glen said. "Like I'm a girl." He stepped aside and yelled at the bear. He said, "Does a bear shit in the woods?"

Two handlers were leading Chip toward his cage, and the one in front of Glen said, "Christ."

Eddie grabbed Glen's arm. Glen shook him off and charged past the handler, who had turned to see what was happening with Chip. The man lunged after Glen, and Glen punched at him. Missed. He crouched, ready to wrestle this guy if that was all they would let him do.

"Jesus H. Christ," the man said. Behind him, the bear dropped to all fours. Another man, part of the crew, hurried over. He said to Eddie, "Get the crazy bastard out of here."

Glen took another swing, and the handler grappled him into

a headlock. Two sacks of sand in a fight. Eddie said, "Get your hands off him." He shoved the guy, and the man let go of Glen. "Back off," Eddie said to him. Glen, hands on his knees, was breathing hard. His face was red. His lips purple.

"I'm going to pin him," Glen said. "Say your prayers and count to three." Glen bull-rushed. Eddie caught him, and they tripped over a pipe and went down, Glen on top. A handler jabbed his boot into Glen's hip, rolled him, and said, "Old-timer, get out of here." Eddie jerked the foot away, and he told the dipshit to back off. The man said, "Get out of here. Both of you."

"He's dying," Eddie said.

The man said, "That ain't no excuse."

"Bootlickers," Glen said. He was lying on his back. Chip the bear was under control. It was going to take half an hour for Glen to get to his feet and put himself in gear.

Late night, Court Street. One-way traffic as if Athens were a big city. Eddie on foot. College kids crowded into the bars. They jaywalked and hounded passers-by. Howled, yelled, getting noticed being one way to respond to the universe and its indifference. Get yourself seen. Haul your t-shirt over your head. Show your tits, ladies. Most of the bars had their doors open, and kids spilled out. There was rock-and-roll. Jazz. Country music. At Lucky's, lost in the crowd, Eddie hogged a booth and sat through a blow-out, *Sunday Night Football,* the Vikings over the Lions by thirty-one.

Eddie drained his beer. He found the head and took a leak. He returned to his table, and there was Kefauver.

"Sit," Kefauver said.

"On my way out," Eddie said. "But you're welcome to my spot."

Kefauver said, "Be cordial."

"There's a word for you," Eddie said.

Mailbox stood to one side of Eddie. The fool who had held the gun at Eddie's head jitterbugged on the other side.

"Buy you a drink?" Eddie said. "Is that what you're saying? Pay you back some of the money I cost you. Or you're going to buy me one. Pay me back, is that it?"

Kefauver said, "However you look at it."

Mailbox said, "It's sixes." As if he knew what he was saying. His talking at all was like he was spitting.

Eddie said, "Not likely." He lit a cigarette. He wasn't going to sit. Not on his life. He moved in close to the fool kid, to the gunslinger—could smell infection on the boy's breath—and he said, "I bet you're good with your hands. You can fix things, right? You studying to be a doctor?" Eddie was dropping smoke on the kid. He said, "Maybe your plan is to be dentist."

Kefauver stood. Like this was a closet. He was taller than Eddie and pressing this fact on him. He said, "Jew boy."

Gunslinger got himself all excited, and he said, "I'm thinking from the look of him maybe he's dipped. Got some Negroid in him. Got him some relatives over there in Bartlett."

"Your eye," Eddie said, and he pointed at Kefauver's. "My God, what is that? There. Right there."

Kefauver said, "What?" He pawed at his eye.

One Mile Past Dangerous Curve   191

"Sucker was twitching," Eddie said. "Is that a sign that you're being fierce?" He stepped aside, tapped Mailbox's arm, and said, "You saw it, didn't you?"

Struck the idiot speechless.

Eddie said, "It could have been the lights. Too bright for a bar, wouldn't you say? Not what you want where you're doing your drinking. I swear, though, it twitched."

Kefauver said, "Listen, Jew boy—"

Eddie said, "You can do better than that."

The man licked his lips.

"Jews," Eddie said, "can't dance." He stepped back, around a couple that chose that second to pass through, and he walked out. There were young men and women everywhere. Eddie waited by the door. He might as well see where this was going. He smoked two Camels. People drifted out, but no Kefauver. No Mailbox. No Gunslinger. A yellow light lay on the brick streets. It softened the shadows.

After midnight, and he walked south on Court Street. At a phone booth, he dialed M&M. Got no answer.

There were dogs on the roam. Educated ones, you could tell. Lank and disciplined. Schooled.

Eddie passed Graffiti Wall on his way to the bridge over the Hocking River. A couple of skateboarders were spray-painting Krazy Kat on the brick. This was the university's property, and as long as you kept your slogans and pontificating and pictorials somewhat clean, you acted with the school's blessing. The skateboarders, done, having roughed in a round cartoon bomb, its fuse lit, near Krazy Kat's foot, like he was playing soccer

192   Darrell Spencer

with it, hit their boards and flew down the sidewalk. One was wearing a do-rag. Both had backpacks.

Three nights of heavy rain had loaded the river's banks. Too late, though. The tomatoes in southeastern Ohio were runts, and the corn was dried on the stalks. All the rain did was bring floods.

Eddie passed the Ohio University Inn. Thought about getting a room for the night.

He found himself back at Glen's.

Nowhere else to be here in Ohio.

There was a light on in the house, and he came upon Glen in the TV room. He was wearing his miracle glasses.

"You okay?" Eddie said.

Nothing from the old guy.

Eddie sat with him until two. It was quiet in the house. He got up to leave, thinking Glen was asleep, and Glen said, "Box my ears. I can deal with it." He rubbed his leg and said, "But don't sandbag me. Fight like a man."

"Me?" Eddie said.

Glen wasn't talking to Eddie. It was a prayer. Glen in conversation with God. "Give me a task to perform," Glen said, "and I'll come through. Go ahead. Test me."

Eddie crouched at his dad's side.

"Square up a ring, and I'll go toe to toe," Glen said.

Sorry, Eddie thought. So sorry.

"But not this," Glen said. "Not this."

Eddie said, "How about you and me and that ride?"

Glen fully registered Eddie's being here. He said, "I'm sitting on death row. You know what I'm saying?"

"Let's go," Eddie said. He got to his feet, offered his father a hand up, and Glen took it.

"Coolville?" Glen said.

Eddie said, "Wherever you want."

"It might work," Glen said. He removed those stupid glasses and said, "It's a possibility, if you pursue the idea to its logical end." He grabbed his map and wrenched himself to his feet, a tug of war between arms and legs and torso. He got into his loafers. He zipped his jumpsuit to his throat. Then he hesitated, slipped out of gear, the showbiz has-been backstage in the wings, Mr. Magic who has been talked out of retirement for one last show, jittery, patting himself down, taking inventory— scarves up his sleeves, check. Levitating wand, check. Doves in coat pockets, still cooing, their tiny hearts ticking. Glen spun the bottle of himself and said, "You're onto something here, if you think about it. They've got an interest in us medically. You hear a lot of reports dealing with the medical aspect. Who knows how far ahead they are? What advances they've made. Hell, the body is mechanical. It's electrical. We know that. You talk about electricity and you're talking rewiring. There's every possibility they have the know-how." He was out the door ahead of Eddie, still talking, fired up. He said, "You get people saying they can't recall what happened. They saw a light. They heard a sound, music like no one on earth can play. Not coming from any instrument known to us. You smell something peculiar. Nothing like what you've ever smelled. You feel a burn. Next thing you know it's days later. Psycholo-

194   Darrell Spencer

gists put them under hypnosis—five out of six times they'll tell you about a physical exam they've been put through."

"What are you talking about?" Eddie said.

"People who've been abducted, they can't tell you where they've been, and they can't tell you how they got back. But you put them under hypnosis—an expert puts them through the steps, and they talk about medical-looking apparatus. They describe lights brighter than what we've got on earth. Experiences beyond what's here on the planet."

Eddie was and wasn't following. Abduction. He got that.

"I'm talking about a cure," Glen said. "These are advanced civilizations. Zap and I'm cancer free. I'm a walking and talking miracle here in Ohio. Only it's science that did it. You got to figure they're thousands of years ahead of us. These are advanced people. They fly spacecraft. But who'd believe me if I announced it that way? Do you think? Huh. We'll give God credit."

They pulled onto the avenue below Glen's. He refused to buckle in. He was squirming in his seat.

"Clap your hands for Jesus," he said. "We'll say I was sitting in the La-Z-Boy, and an angel of the Lord walked in like he was strolling into a restaurant. He puts his hands on me, and he heals me."

"You've come a long way from UFOs," Eddie said.

Glen said, "You'll witness for me. God works in mysterious ways his wonders to perform."

There was not a soul on the streets. Glen told Eddie to take 682 to 56. He was playing a hunch. He was hearing a voice in his ear. They weren't driving to Coolville. Glen was thinking it

One Mile Past Dangerous Curve   195

was a different night. They would try a different bridge. "We got two choices," he said to Eddie, his map open on his lap, the truck's overhead light on. "I'm guessing Cox Bridge." He tapped the map, and he said, "I'm thinking it's isolated. Off the beaten path. I've got me a feeling."

"Go to 93, you're saying?"

"It's a test," Glen said. "Am I smart enough I deserve them?"

"Sort of like hide-and-seek?"

"South off 93. Not far." Glen folded up his map and turned off the light. He rolled down his window. "Where we're going, it's a crossroads," Glen said. "You can't say they don't have a sense of humor."

Eddie drove, spent time thinking on what he would report to M&M. One more ride through the heartland. In spite of a full moon, this journey was so dark it was like driving in Glen's Natural Vision USA glasses. She would acknowledge Eddie was being brave. God only knew what was happening outside to his right and to his left. There in the woods. Now and then he spotted a house window lit yellow from behind a shade. The old Toyota accepted the turns, and Glen fell asleep. Mile after mile, rolling hills, steep, and banked, and at the bottom thick fog. It gathered the headlights into a wall, and Eddie braked. He slowed enough he feared capture. On flat land, the fog collected oncoming lights and swirled them.

The night sky was purple, as deeply colored as an eggplant. Smooth and flat. The moon—to the east? West? God, but Eddie had no idea. He was so discombobulated he could have run into himself. There hung that full moon. It was orange, sitting here and saying you could drive over and park under it if doing so would help you. Bring your lunch. Have a picnic. Your dog is welcome, but on a leash only.

Hill-and-valley driving. Crooked roads. That was it. All the talking he had done trying to tell M&M what it was like here.

Crooked roads, M&M. There you go.

He couldn't find a pen to make a note. He would remember. Had to.

Crooked roads.

They entered Zaleski State Forest. There was a sign at the outskirts. FOREST CLOSES AT TEN. Sure. Why not? New Plymouth, population 565, coming up. Eddie blew through. Not a light on. Not a car in sight.

He slowed for 93 and was thinking he should go left, but he had confused north south east and west so many times here in Ohio he was wishing Glen awake. Like every other trip he had taken in this state the drive could easily have turned him around.

"You go left," Glen said.

Eddie did.

The covered bridge was half a mile down the highway, off to the right, up a side road. It and a new steel bridge stood side by side. Eddie parked in front of a sign. BRIDGE CLOSED. *Pain* was hand-lettered in black across the words. Two cement posts kept you from driving across, from testing the planks in a vehicle. The roof was tin, and there was open space between the side-walls and it. Light shone through. You could walk over to the covered bridge. It would hold foot traffic.

Eddie said, "Is that it?"

"It must be," Glen said. He didn't budge, but rolled his window shut and asked Eddie to kill the lights. Glen settled into the truck seat. He said, "I'm thinking we sit and wait. They'll come."

"Should I blink the lights?" Eddie said. It was a bad joke at the wrong time. He said, "We'll see them?"

"Not likely."

"What, then?"

"Don't talk," Glen said. "Don't say a word. If I disappear, don't stick around. They'll return me. Even if it's days. You go on ahead home, and then come back if I haven't figured out how to get there. Don't tell Joy. She doesn't need to know."

"Don't tell her what?"

"Anything. Me being cured, for one. Which she won't believe even if I outlive her."

"What if I come back without you?" Eddie said. He caught himself. He had bought into this stupidity.

"You can make something up," Glen said.

"Like?"

"Use your head."

Eddie walked over to the bridge. Woods all around. He stepped on the planks. Solid. Halfway through, he stopped. His eyes adjusted, and in the moonlight he saw names carved into the wooden supports.

Hirsch.

Willie.

Buffie.

Then two names, and a heart between them. Someone

hearted someone. What a thing to know here in the middle of the night in Ohio.

You had to kneel to carve the names. So Eddie did. Three rules for a sign painter. Always carry a rag. Always carry a lighter. Always carry a knife. He opened his, sat himself into a catcher's squat, and couldn't think of one damn thing he wanted to carve.

Not one damn thing.

Then he cut *M&M* into the wood. She would love it. He couldn't wait to tell her. Maggie's name here in a covered bridge in Ohio. He didn't want a photo. Just the telling. She would love his telling her about what he had done.

Glen was asleep. Comes with the territory, Eddie thought. He lit a Camel and rolled down his window. Glen slept through the night and woke only when the sun lit the trees. The dawn was that pretty that knocked your socks into next week. The red and yellow and blue of bushes intensified. Eddie backed down the road and onto the highway. Drove to 93. They would be home in little over an hour.

The other shoe had dropped. Glen, who had always been as headstrong and grim as celibacy, who had spent his adult life firewalking from petulant and snappish to cross and sore-headed, had now undergone his own brand of the last straw, and he had come out the other side a wreck. Circles could no longer be counted on to be round. No more parachutes were going to open in the nick of time. Nothing would ever again fulfill the measure of its creation. Up to now the big worry of his getting older had been false teeth and his hearing. He had lost high-pitched sound in his left ear. He had seen what false teeth did to a man. Glen swore he would put a gun to his head before he would live with dentures floating in a glass next to his bed. His hearing (back in Las Vegas the diagnosis, which was only a guess, was he had had a stroke that had affected his left ear)—he had driven six hours and asked the Miracle Ear people in L.A., *Will I get it back?* Their reply: *We won't say you won't. You'd make a liar out of us.* So Glen loaded up on their vitamin B-12 (the promise of increased blood flow) and waited for sound to return the way you finally locate a radio station that has been out of range. Then came the Big C. Glen hadn't seen that coming down the pike.

Cancer beyond repair. Say what you want about blood tests, remission or regression, about a falling PSA count, clear MRIs and sonograms, the Big C didn't throw up its hands, lower its head and skulk away. It had the will and instincts of a stalker. It had all your phone numbers, past present and future, listed and unlisted. It had your address. It knew every route you took to work.

Glen planted himself in his La-Z-Boy. Firmly. Like a nut to a bolt. Like anger in its Sunday suit. He didn't leave the house. He ate from a tray, if he ate at all.

Three days.

Five.

A week.

R & R. A reprieve. A.J. and Eddie were driving to Marietta. They planned to circle back along the Ohio River. Hoped to explore Portsmouth and the Roy Rogers Museum. A.J. was telling Eddie he needed to see where George Washington camped above the Great Hockhocking River. He ought to put a toe in the river itself. There was an island they could ferry to, a castle on it, built by Aaron Burr or Jefferson or Monroe or Alexander somebody, one of those founding fathers on the lam.

They located Highway 550, known nationally as a biker's dream, and Eddie found the Tappet Brothers on the radio.

Everywhere hills and meadows were laid out like a gorgeous dress. Sumac. Willows. Cotton had told A.J. he heard campers had spotted black bears south of Athens. The TV news people were saying, "Respect them for what they are. Animals." Eddie and A.J. cruised by barns and sheds that seemed to be leaning into a wind and holding onto their hats. Long gone, the Shawnee, the Cherokee, Delaware, the Wyandot. There was a herd of buffalo outside Albany, fenced against the Appalachian Highway.

One stipulation today: no family talk.

No woe.

No family shit.

"You a camper?" A.J. wondered.

Eddie said, "Only in motels."

"Thank God," she said.

"Love motels," he said. "Don't you?"

She said, "Mostly the decor. Particularly the furniture."

"Exactly. Of course."

What they saw of the sky, when the woods released them and the trees gave way to lowlands, made Eddie long for the West. It was a spectacular, impossible blue. A color you might see on tiles poolside.

On the radio, banjo music, and the Tappet Brothers' opening bit, a rehash of an ongoing subject—*last words,* those spoken in the few seconds before an untimely death. Listeners were sending in their favorites, and Frick and Frack were having the time of their lives. First, a classic: *What's this button for?* Then, *Nice doggie.* One right out of a local newspaper somewhere in Nebraska: *Watch this.* There was a direct quote: *We was lowering the thing toward the river, and he said, "Watch this."* One from a couple out of Ohio: *What could be simpler? Red to red, black to black.*

The brothers solved a problem for a lady named Deborah, the seven-letter spelling, not the five. Her ignition key stuck. Was hard to turn. "Grip the steering wheel tight," Frick said. "Rattle it, back and forth."

"The key?" she said.

Frack said, "The wheel. The steering column."

Deborah said, "Then what?"

"Turn the key at the same time," Frick said.

"Rattle the steering wheel and turn the key?" she said.

Frack said, "Walk and chew gum."

Frick said, "Rub your head and pat your stomach."

She said, "Grip, rattle and turn."

Frick and Frack said, "You got it."

"That's it?" she said. "That's your expert advice?"

Frack said, "Don't be afraid to be angry with it."

Frick said, "Shake rattle and roll."

"Left and right," Frack said. "Jiggle it."

"So much of life," Frick said, "is knowing how tough to be."

Frack said, "Sure. Is knowing when to whack something."

"Is understanding when to take the five-pound sledgehammer to the brake drum."

"Or the TV."

Second caller was a man with a groaning Lexus. He had no sense of humor. Next guy liked popping his car out of gear—no clutch. Their advice? Stop it, exclamation point. Frack asked a woman if she worked at a flower shop. No. Did she use a cream rinse? No. "Would you like to?" he said. Her problem resulted in a debate, Frack saying, "I like spark," and Frick saying, "I like fuel pump."

"What's left?" Frack said.

Frick said, "Air. Earth. Fire."

Frack said, "I'm thinking the t-word."

"Not the t-word."

"Yup."

"Transmission."

They debated the spelling of Betty, B-e-t-t-y or B-e-t-t-e, Frack saying you don't throw away a spelling because it's not commonly used.

A woman complained of squishy brakes. She said, "Not always squishy, but sometimes squishy and sometimes not." She lived in New Jersey. Their advice? Move. Always picking on New Jersey, Frick and Frack, those Boston boys.

Frick said to her, "Was it cloudy when this happened?"

"I see where you're going with this," Frack said.

"Had it rained?"

It had rained. Sure enough. It had rained, and it was overcast. The Tappet Brothers to the rescue.

Eddie followed his nose and drove across what he thought was the Ohio River but would learn later was not. M&M, that night—he phoned from Marietta—double-checked her maps and quizzed him. What he had driven over turned out to be dinky water by comparison, was a tributary, the Muskingum. She asked him if he was going east or west. He couldn't say. "Where was the sun?" M&M said. He was too busy driving to know. M&M said, "Close your eyes. Think back. Imagine yourself on the bridge. Can you feel the sun? On a shoulder? On your neck?" He couldn't. "Jeeez," M&M said. Whatever he had done he and A.J. drove into town. They lunched, and then walked along the bank of the Ohio on stones laid out like a patio. Seventy degrees. A breeze and no humidity you noticed. That white film that seemed always to set itself against the sky was missing. The day fooled Eddie into thinking this was a livable place. They met a couple and their three dogs, one a black poodle-mix who must have been a statesman in an early incarnation. Eddie crouched and held the dog's face. The dog had eyes like he had talk with Aristotle, Plato, Buddha. You name it. He understood what there was to understand about Western thought. About chance. About design and disorder. There was dignity in the way the dog held himself. Their white terrier—named Eddie like Eddie—fought to stay in the water. The dog had it in his head he might swim the Ohio for the sport of it. Bicyclers passed behind A.J. and Eddie.

A paddle boat came up the river. Sternwheeler—A.J. corrected Eddie. It occurred to him he wasn't sure whether or not they did cross the Ohio River. He assumed they had.

A.J. pointed. "That's West Virginia," she said.

Twirl Eddie around. He said, "No. We're still in Ohio?"

She said, "We are."

He looked past an island. Sure enough. Trees, shoreline. A boat cutting by. He searched for the sun, and there it squatted. Clearly in the wrong place. It had made a mistake.

They drove over to West Virginia, stood in line and bought a Power Ball lottery ticket. One only. A.J.'s rule. One ticket, a thousand tickets—same odds. She kissed it for luck. One hundred and fifty-six million dollars up for grabs. They toured a glass factory. The place made gazing balls, a phenomenon Eddie sensed he misunderstood. He walked up to them in yards where they posed on their pedestals. They shimmered, reflecting the world in red or blue or green or silver. Distorting it like a funhouse mirror. Eddie wanted to knock on the door, say, "Why?" and point at the gazing ball. More than that he wanted a decent answer.

Back to Marietta, he and A.J. crossed the Ohio near Williamstown. They lucked into a room at the Lafayette. Got a great view of the river. They made love, conventionally and then like strangers who would never see each other again, once standing up, once sitting down, and once in a four-poster George and Martha might have done it in.

Three A.M., Eddie outside, on the sidewalk above the river. Years ago, married to Patty, but having not seen her for three days, he stopped in the middle of the highway between Tonopah and Las Vegas and walked into the Mojave Desert.

One Mile Past Dangerous Curve   205

He got stuck. He couldn't move. Had felt the fear they say puts a finger on your heart. Now it was here again where he stood near the banks of the Ohio River.

Glen. Joy. Matthew and Mark.

Family shit.

You can't step away from it.

A.J. found him, and they picked their way down the shoreline. The moon lay on the water.

She said, "You slipped out on me."

He said, "I hadn't seen anything like this until I came here."

"The river?" she said.

Yeah.

"Here," she said, and she put her arm around his waist and walked him into the water. Not far. Not far at all. What he understood was that there was a point where if he took one more step there would be no talking to the river. It would take him.

A.J. said, "There's no running from the family, is there?"

"You can run but you can't hide," Eddie said. "Is that biblical? Is that in the Bible?"

A.J. said, "We'll ask Dad. He'll know."

"Yeah," Eddie said. "Maybe I'll paint one sign for myself and post it in the middle of the woods."

Morning, and the Layfette's bread and omelets lived up to their hype. Then it was some towns called Gravel Bank and Constitution. Eddie and A.J. followed the river. Through Belpre to Little Hocking and on to Hockingport, site where, sure enough, a marker told them, George Washington camped November 7, 1777. Washington slept here.

"No mention of Elvis," Eddie said.

So it went.

They walked where the Battle of Buffington took place.

And then at a bend in the Ohio, in an open field between Long Bottom and Hazael, there was one of the signs Eddie had painted for Cotton. Fifteen feet off the road, tall windblown purple wildflowers all around it. No place to pull over. Not a problem. Eddie and A.J. were the only traffic. Eddie parked and got out. A.J. too. COUNT YOUR BLESSINGS.

He held onto to her. Tight.

If ever he could get beyond Patty, here was A.J.

Here was smart. Here was beauty. What could be easier. Here was someone Eddie wanted to be with. He had one thousand and one questions to ask her—it would take a lifetime to get through all of them, and he knew her answers would not pretend to be anything other than what they were.

They reached Pomeroy in time for burgers and fries at McDonald's on the river. Horrible thought Eddie couldn't shake was that *Eyewitness News,* a day or two ago, reported boots discovered on a side street in Pomeroy. Right in the middle of the road. Feet inside them. Feet sawed off a few inches above the ankle. Socks still on.

He kept that picture to himself. A.J. didn't need it.

Their metal table overlooked the Ohio River. A barge, tugboats front and back, made the bend at Pomeroy by taking it in angles, not in an arc, but piecemeal. Eddie stopped eating to watch. No way could the barge get the job done. The turn wasn't a turn but a sectioning. He would describe it all to M&M, and she would research the size of the barge, the tugboats, the river itself, and tell him how such a feat was accomplished.

No time, so A.J. and Eddie gave thumbs-down to Portsmouth. To the Roy Rogers Museum, A.J. saying, "You really want to see Trigger stuffed?" It was getting late. Their weekend spent. They had dawdled. They hadn't missed an antique store. The truck bed was full of chairs and tables and wooden boxes. A.J. needed to get back and Trigger wasn't going anywhere.

It was getting dark when they reached Athens.

"Are you going to hold the fort down?" Eddie said to Roscoe. Roscoe sat like Roscoe. Mute. Eddie lit a Camel. It was three A.M. and getting too cold to be sitting here at night. Eddie had put a jacket on. He had a plan, Stan. To shut things down, to pack, and be gone in a week. He had talked to A.J., and she was thinking on the idea of her coming out. Quitting at the school in December.

"I've got a place," he said to her. "Ten minutes to Lake Mead. You like to swim?"

She said, "In motel pools."

"Me, too."

"Lakes are untamed," she said. "There's too much responsibility."

Now, in the house, the kitchen light came on.

Eddie's time with A.J. had been good. Now he would be punished. A couple of days getting addicted to A.J., and Eddie didn't want to run into Glen. Half hour, three Camels later, the light was still on. He had to go inside.

"Big mistake," Eddie said to Roscoe, and he headed for the slider. He expected Glen, but it was Joy, sitting at the kitchen table. The coffeemaker behind her was ticking, gurgling. Her short hair was wet, and she was dabbing at it with a towel. Eddie thought of Cotton's sign. CAN'T SLEEP? TRY TALKING TO THE SHEPHERD RATHER THAN COUNTING SHEEP.

"What's going on?" Eddie said.

Joy had nothing to give him. He poured coffee, and she told him she spent two hours cleaning up the hallway. Glen didn't get out of bed in time to make it to the bathroom. She heard him bang into a bookcase and found him sitting in a doorway. Shit trailing down the hall. It was loose and bloody. He had stepped in it, and it was smashed into the carpet. He urinated on himself. She flipped a light on, and he asked her to *please turn it off. Please.* They huddled together, in the dark, in the smell, for what had to be that real thing we call eternity. Then she helped Glen up, the smell overwhelming, and she walked him to the shower. Scrubbed him down. Soaked herself. She was helping him into bed and saw he had wet it. She sat him on a chair and changed the sheets. Then it was the floor. It had to be scrubbed. Rinsed. Rescrubbed. Only a new carpet would solve the problem.

She couldn't handle the smell. Got sick herself.

The washing machine off the kitchen was running. Outside the yard lights snapped on, and deer wandered by. "They come through the sliding glass doors," Joy said to Eddie. "Next door had it happen to them."

Eddie had heard that.

"The woman up the street—one fell in her pool."

"What happened?" Eddie said. "Did it die? Drown?"

One Mile Past Dangerous Curve   209

Joy didn't know. She thought they called the police, and the police got in touch with the wildlife people. She said to Eddie, "A pool around here. Does that surprise you as much as it does me?" She folded her towel and set it on the table. "I took a shower," she said.

Eddie said, "It's time to get some help."

"We need to get him home."

"You think we can?"

"Eddie," she said, "I don't want him to die here. He doesn't want to die here."

"I can drive him," Eddie said. He told her he was going. Was thinking one week, but could go tomorrow if that would help. He could leave in five minutes if she chose to. Joy rubbed her foot. The toes had cramped, and she was trying to get them to straighten out. Eddie said, "You sure can't be driving him. Not with those feet."

She said, "He can fly. But quick. He can't wait."

Eddie said, "There are private jets. You can hire them."

"Hire one," Joy said.

Eddie watched her massage her toes.

"He dies here," she said, "and I'm going to have to live with that for the rest of my life."

First call, then, was to Patty. Middle of the night in Las Vegas. "That's terrible news," she said. It was close to six in Ohio. Eddie could have waited, but she wasn't punishing him. She had picked up the phone and said, "Eddie, this has got to be you. What's wrong?"

He told her about Glen. About Joy wanting to get him home.

210   Darrell Spencer

"Can he travel?" Patty said.

Eddie said he was thinking there had to be some kind of small plane they could hire. The university owned an airport. If Joy could get him to Columbus, then she and Glen could be in Las Vegas before the sun set.

Patty said, "Joy's coming with him?"

"I hope so," Eddie said. "They could go together."

"Is there a reason for her to stay?"

"None I can see, unless it's to get away from him."

Patty said she would pick them up.

Then M&M was on the extension, and Patty said to her that her father had good news and bad news. Patty hung up, saying, "Let me know. I'll handle this end."

"Give me the bad first," M&M said to Eddie.

There you go. A true Dancer. Was what Eddie would have said. You got two sides to your face. One's easy to shave. The other's difficult. Which do you shave first? The hard side. No question. The hard side. Always the hard side. Get the tough stuff out of the way.

So he gave her the bad news. Told her her grandfather was in trouble, was dying, and they were making plans to get him home. He withheld the rest of it—what Joy had just been through, the gun, the bear, the UFOs. The family shit that had come home to roost.

M&M said, "The good news?"

"Your pop's on his way home, too."

"That is good news," she said.

Which was when he told her he had taken his final drive here in Ohio, the one to Marietta, oldest city in the northwest terri-

One Mile Past Dangerous Curve   211

tory. He filled her in. Eddie made standing alongside the Ohio River sound like at least the eighth wonder of the world as far as experiences went. He outdid himself describing the highway he and A.J. drove. Eddie used words like *coiled* and *plunged* and *pitched*. *Sloggy*. *Grind*. Even said *shortcoming, miscarried* and *gone astray*. Then he remembered. He said, "Crooked." He said, "Crooked beyond repair." *Detours?* she said. He said *shrouded* and *eclipsed*. He threw in *fear of highjacking*, hinting at the danger, sublimating the robbery he had lived through.

He thought about the feet in the boots on the street in Pomeroy, there by the Ohio River.

"Eddie," she said, "Eddie, you have to do me one more favor."

"Anything, Pumpkin."

"Don't talk like that, Eddie."

He did know better. Wondered where that had come from. He was outside, had returned to the redwood table, Roscoe still by his side. The toad was giving him a look like he didn't recognize this fool. Eddie offered the toad a cigarette. He said to M&M, "What's the favor?"

Did Eddie know where the Ridges was? The old state hospital. Of course. He drove by three, four times a day. The highway beneath the buildings followed the Hocking River. "Great," she said. Here's what Eddie was to do. Go there, right now.

"It's after six in the morning here," he said. "Going on seven."

"So much the better."

"It's foggy. It's kind of cold."

212   Darrell Spencer

"Perfect."

"It's low clouds and getting ready to rain. The drought's over. We've got fields washed out."

M&M wanted him to imagine a thousand gibbering patients. The moans. The groans. The shuffling about. She understood the buildings had been sealed. The Internet told her that. A website told her about the art gallery and buildings being refurbished. Told her there was no entrance to the old rooms.

"You'll find a way in," M&M said. "Sealed is the point of all this. Scary. Frightening. We're talking about you overcoming basic fears, Eddie." She said, "Put your thinking cap on. You saw the pentagram. You're safe."

She told Eddie that when the city was closing down the hospital, one patient, a woman everyone called Baby Louise, sneaked in for a keepsake she had left behind. One story had it that it was her father's pocket watch. Another said it was a necklace and locket, a photo of her twin brother inside. The twin had died at birth. Baby Louise was deaf and mute. The twin had stolen her voice and her hearing and carried them off to the grave. She wandered the halls, and the workers sealed her wing shut. Trapped her. She didn't hear. She couldn't talk. She was wearing only a nightgown. M&M told Eddie to imagine her terror. To picture her at a window, but this was a top floor, and no one was looking up. The workers packed away their gear and left.

Eddie said, "That sounds like hooey."

Baby Louise starved slowly, the way an ant would. Mute. Deaf. Silent. Hungry. They found her decomposed body months later, her bones curled into a fetal position around her keepsake, the watch, the locket, the photo and memory of her twin. The two of them had shared a womb. Now they shared death. Her body left a stain, and her spirit wandered the grave-yard in the woods behind the Ridges. She carried a lantern and hummed.

M&M said, "At the entrance to her wing you'll see scrawled in blood the words *Welcome to Hell*."

He said, "You're pulling your dad's leg and scaring him to boot."

"They paint over the words, but, of course, that does no good. The letters bleed through no matter what color they use," M&M said. "The words drip blood."

"What is it you're sending your father to do?" Eddie said.

"You're safe, Eddie," she said.

"You're not answering the question."

"You'll be okay."

"Why wasn't she, then, the deaf woman?" he said. "Why wasn't she safe?"

M&M said, "Don't be logical, Eddie. Be brave."

"What is it I'm doing?" he said.

She said, "They've scrubbed at the stain, and they can't remove it. You'll see it, the shape of her body, curled up, fetal."

"Why?" he said.

"Don't ask why, Eddie. Be brave."

"What's the point?"

"There is no point, Eddie. Your daughter's curious, is all. Pictures can be faked. On the Internet, in real life. You're going to see all of it and tell me about the stain, the letters."

Next, he phoned Noah. "Shit," was Olive Root's greeting.

214   Darrell Spencer

"I need to talk to Noah," Eddie said.

Olive Root said, "Shit. It's dark out." Noah in the background, talking at her, saying, "Is that about the boys? Who is it?"

Eddie filled Noah in. Could he arrange for a plane? For Glen and Joy. No problem. He would get on it. They could fly Glen and Joy to Columbus. From there to Las Vegas. Be home this afternoon.

Noah said, "This is what I was talking about. You see. I saw it coming."

"You, me, Snapper, business, none of it is the issue right now," Eddie said. "It'll take care of itself."

Noah said, "Nothing takes care of itself, Eddie. We're not talking about peanuts."

Eddie said, "Noah, let's get him home."

Then Eddie drove over to the Ridges. No sleep going on two days now. All this trouble with Glen, and still he was keeping his promise to his daughter. Why? Because M&M was his kid.

Lights still lit up the bike trail along the Hocking River. Ugly black clouds were low enough to touch. A brick road wound him to the top of the ridge, where Eddie parked. Old iron stairways zig-zagged up the sides of the interlocking buildings. There were two turrets at the center and, above the main entrance, balconies, tiers of them. Gothic as a word or a concept or a way of thinking didn't cover the horror Eddie was looking at. Rows of windows, hundreds of them, all lined up, all framed and held in check by decorative iron work. No jumping allowed. A truck came up a road to the right, from the rear end of the buildings. It turned into a parking lot, reversed and

One Mile Past Dangerous Curve   215

stopped. Sat idling, puffing exhaust. The cab was white. The bed, dark, an ugly brown. Rain fell hard. There was no way for Eddie to get inside the place. He followed the brick road, and it circled him around and past the museum. He slowed at a bend and glanced at his rearview mirror. Headlights behind him, someone hesitating at the turn. There was a building that looked like a chapel. There were cottages. A delivery dock. The road led Eddie to a choice, go straight ahead, or turn. He horseshoed onto the switchback, and above him, where he had been, was the truck. Eddie ended up at an intersection, Highway 682 and Richland Avenue. Richland would take him back to Glen's. He pulled into a gas station, and the truck drove on by. A piece-of-shit sign pasted to the gas pumps said, WE FILL YOU UP FOR SELF-SERVE PRICES.

Eddie ignored it. He filled the tank and wondered what he would tell M&M. He had not seen a lantern, of course. No diaphanous lady walking about. No lights in windows. Getting inside wasn't even an option. But he would satisfy her. Eddie would give his daughter part of what she wanted. He would pull her leg completely off and put it on backwards. Eddie would tell her how he had walked up the thirteen steps to the main door.

"Thirteen?" she would say.

"Well, twelve," he would say. "Then twelve-A."

"Thirteen's a lucky number."

"Of course."

She would then tell him about the queen who declared the number thirteen not only sacred, but the number women hold dearest. Eve invented the number. Gave torturous birth to it.

216   Darrell Spencer

Truth would be Eddie didn't get out of the truck. Which was fine. A building is a building. M&M would learn that and similar lessons soon enough.

"Did you go inside?" she would say.

He would tell her it was closed. Was all locked up. There were chains and padlocks. But he would hint that he heard pounding, the sound of fists beating on a door. Then there were footsteps. He would say he saw a cloaked figure descend a stairway, stoop low, look Eddie's way, then flee.

"Eddie," she would say, "there would be somehow to get in."

No, Pumpkin. Not this morning. If there was, he didn't want to find it. Eddie had hands to shake. Babies to kiss. A father to load into a plane, even if they had to deliver him in his La-Z-Boy.

The truck Eddie saw behind him was idling in a stall in a car wash, its headlights off, facing Richland. Eddie braked and cut sharply into the parking lot. He climbed out of the Toyota, and the truck reversed out of the stall and took off.

A pretty to make you lightheaded and inexact. No denying it. One gorgeous place, this Ohio. These hills. The colors of fall. God's green earth turning in upon itself, the exchange of beauty for beauty. Being the sign painter he was, Eddie could have put words to the array but doing so would have been an insult.

Ten A.M. Eddie sat on the redwood table. Break time. He and Noah had spent the morning getting Joy and Glen ready to

One Mile Past Dangerous Curve   217

leave. They located a pilot who would fly Glen and Joy to Columbus. They packed two suitcases. Joy wasn't up to it. Glen, definitely not. Eddie lit a Camel. Sipped at coffee. No sleep since his and A.J.'s trip.

No Roscoe this morning, which wasn't unusual. The toad a creature of the night. Some time ago, Joy had discovered baby toads in the high grasses. Roscoe's dirty little secret. Roscoe was a she not a he. Eddie told M&M one night, and she said, "The babies nurture in a clutch. If Roscoe is the kind of toad we guess he is, he protects them by clinging to the sac. He does hands-on bodyguarding to keep predators away."

"You looked this up?" Eddie said.

She said, "I'm on the computer as we speak."

Quiet this morning. The squirrels on tiptoe.

In the top of a tree were sleek gray-brown birds, traveling, it seemed, together. Subtle, if birds could be said to be such a thing. A quarter inch of tail dipped in yellow. One of Joy's hedgerows overnight had traded green for a flaming red. A jay screeched, baboonlike. More shriek than bird call. Eddie would not have been overly surprised and half-expected to see Glen in a leopard-skin loincloth and carrying a spear come swinging sycamore to sycamore through the back yards.

But Glen, the man who seldom drank, had gotten into the bourbon early in the morning and landed in the La-Z-Boy. No one had told him yet what was afoot. He slept. He woke. He snored. He woke, and he yelled at the universe. Cursed God, the land, the sun, the stars and the moon. Bellowed. He declared that he would eat snakes if he thought it would do any good. Then dropped into stupor, which he drifted in and out of. Eddie

218   Darrell Spencer

dumped half the bourbon down the sink and hauled the rest of the liquor to his trailer.

Glen urinated where he sat. The room smelled like mangy dog. Sour. Fetid. One of those early-morning talk shows filled the house. People badgering each other. The host insipid. The past mattering more than it needed to, as if all sorrow and hatred had its roots in affronts and insults suffered when you were two or three years old. Glen's cicada photographs had begun to fall to the floor. There were gaps in the rows, and the pictures lay on the tile. Joy refused to touch them. A point she was making. She passed by the downstairs slider, carrying her notepad, listing what Eddie was to give to Re-Used Industries, what he could sell with the house, what the Salvation Army would take. Her plants went to a neighbor. She didn't want one item from this place coming to Las Vegas. She had shown Eddie what she was doing. "Read it," she said. He did. *Don't send anything* underlined twice.

The plan. A flight out of the university airport delivered Joy and Glen to Columbus International this afternoon. It was scheduled to leave at one. They left Columbus at six, private plane. Patty and M&M were set to pick them up in Las Vegas. Noah and Olive Root would drive to Columbus and meet them. Help them at the airport. Send them off.

The big hitch was Glen. How to get him on his feet. Showered. Dressed. In shoes. How to tell him they were going. They had to figure out how to keep Glen from being Glen.

Noah and Olive Root came to drive Glen and Joy to the university airport. Then they would head for Columbus. Olive Root was reason enough for Eddie to be outside. Sorry to think

One Mile Past Dangerous Curve   219

it, and, God, he wished he hadn't, but she was one person who needed her tongue cut out. He lit a Camel from a Camel. His truck, one last sign for Cotton loaded in the bed, was parked out front in the driveway. Mother whitetail and her twins high-stepped along the ridge. A twin spotted Eddie. Froze, and the mother sensed its fear. She stared directly at Eddie. Blew air through her nose. Stamped a foot.

Eddie said, "Fresh flowers out front."

Tails high, and they were gone. Folklore on the move.

From inside the house, Glen was shouting. "You say so," he said.

Time for Eddie to get off his butt. He looked through the slider and saw Olive Root standing in the doorway of the kitchen. She shifted hair side to side. Looked today like she was wearing a poodle for a wig. She stepped to one side, and Noah brushed by her. Hesitated. He saw Eddie and gave him a wild stare.

Adios. Noah and Eddie had been through the I-told-you-so's, Eddie retreating to his position—the business, all Noah's. His to handle. His to dig out from under. Eddie circled the porch and the side of the house. He didn't see the trouble until he got to the Toyota. Kefauver. A truck blocking the driveway, a Jeep to one side of it, slanted in, winch attached to the front, roll bar, camouflaged brown and green. In the back of the truck, standing tall and being counted, Matthew and Mark. The mirrored sunglasses Eddie had seen when he got robbed. Rifles, pointed down. Such good boys. Such safety nuts. Their shirts opened on tattoos on their chests, skulls, each a bony eye-socketed head smoking a cigar, one pointed left and one pointed right. Surely the boys would be wearing combat boots. A Chevy Impala parked on the other side of the truck. Restored, vintage sixties—tailfins to make a space cadet jealous.

Kefauver eased himself out of the passenger's side of the Impala. Next came Mailbox. Then Gunslinger, who was toting a revolver.

Danger on them like sweat.

So much it was all kind of funny.

Kefauver was dressed like one of those generals you see on a battlefield, an army-green t-shirt, big pants tucked into boots. Dog tags swinging. The man would eat tin before he would cry uncle. He wasn't showing a weapon. Matthew and Mark hopped down from the truck, and two shaved-headed jackasses got out of the Jeep, ponytails the only hair they had, plugged in low to the neck at the back. One retrieved a rifle from a gun rack.

It was all silly. And frightening.

Eddie stayed behind the tailgate.

Kefauver got close enough, and he said to Eddie, "You own yourself a nice home, sign man." Got nothing from Eddie. This was Kefauver's show. Somewhere in a house among the trees someone was dialing 911. Gunslinger came around the front of the Toyota, the fool walking like he was moving cross-legged through tires.

"Sweet peas," Eddie said.

Gunslinger stopped.

"You don't want to hurt the sweet peas," Eddie said. "To your left. Be careful of the sweet peas. You might fall."

The fool raised his revolver. Aimed it at Eddie's chest. Odd

One Mile Past Dangerous Curve   221

result was he put himself in jeopardy. Like there was no way the pistol could do anything but explode in the kid's face.

Eddie said, "You ought to be apologizing."

Gunslinger glanced at Kefauver, who said to Eddie, "Jew boy—"

Eddie was out from behind the truck, was out from the backside of the sign, and moving toward Kefauver, seeing out of the corner of his eye the arm, the revolver, and at the most seventy-five points of IQ tracking him. Somehow it calmed Eddie. It was, truly, all so silly. He said to Kefauver, "You limit your vocabulary, sir, you limit your response to the world." He was going to salute, but understood Gunslinger's gun could go off on its own if he did.

Kefauver wasn't looking at Eddie. But past him. Eddie heard, "Glen." Joy's cry. Something up behind him.

Here came Glen, jumpsuit stained two, three times over on both sides of the crotch. No shoes, parboiled feet and face. White hair like ragweed. Carriage, though, like this really was what it was, a showdown. Glen had been right. Someone up above had a sense of humor. God or aliens, it didn't matter. At Glen's side, there by the leg he no longer owned, the gimpy one—a six-shooter right out of the Old West.

Matthew and Mark were also on the move, coming forward. They had set their rifles on the grass and were trotting.

Gunslinger swung his arm, gun on Glen, then on Eddie, then on Kefauver, then gun on Matthew and Mark. Eddie's only fear was confusion might cause the idiot to shoot someone. Noah appeared in the front door of the house, and Joy stepped behind him. Olive Root was on a cell phone. Noah said, "Mark.

222   Darrell Spencer

Matthew." The boys stopped. They looked at Noah the way the twin deer had looked at Eddie.

"Who are you?" Glen said to Kefauver. "What do you want?"

Kefauver got into a patch pocket at the thigh of his military pants. He produced his own pistol. Small as a lady's hand.

Fucking-a, silly had become sillier.

This was crazy.

This was nuts.

Kefauver said, "We have business." He nodded at Eddie.

"Business?" Glen said. He kept coming at Kefauver. "You have sign business, and you bring guns? What? My boy cheated you? I don't think so. Not my boy. Nope. Didn't happen. I'm not believing my boy cheated you."

"It's not sign business," Kefauver said. He signaled for Gunslinger to lower his gun. A good-sense move.

"What kind of business brings you to my property carrying guns and acting like the world isn't a civilized place?"

"It's between us. Me and the Jew boy."

"The what?"

"Me and your son. We have a conflict."

"No," Glen said. "You brought weapons. You brought guns. You blocked off a free and open driveway."

"Old man—"

"Old man." Glen had gotten to within a foot of Kefauver. No way could Kefauver raise the gun to shoot. "I could act crazy," Glen said. "I could act like I think you've come to take me to a loony bin. I'll holler about them bringing the straitjackets."

"Old man—"

"Say it again," Glen said.

Eddie said, "Dad."

"No no no," Glen said.

Noah was coming down the front walk, easy on his feet, like he was getting into a boat on a lake. He was headed toward Mark and Matthew. They had stopped, unsure about which way to step. Right. Left. Forward. Backwards. This wasn't what they had signed on for.

Glen said, "Not dad. Old man. Ask the doctor here. This fool wearing army clothes."

Kefauver started walking away, backwards, facing Glen.

"Doctor, doctor," Glen said. "My dick won't work. Can you help me?"

Kefauver stopped and waved for Gunslinger, Mailbox, the others to get into their vehicles. Matthew and Mark stood where they were. Noah waved them toward him, but they didn't move.

"Penile implant," Glen said.

Kefauver said, "This has nothing to do with you. It—"

"It does," Glen said. He limped closer to Kefauver. "It does, it does," he said. "Old man, you say. I'm an old man can't get it up. But—here's a big but for you. I can give you what you want."

Ten years later, in the desert, Eddie, waiting on paint to dry, sitting on the tailgate of a truck, would once again see this moment. He thought he saw the gun come up in Glen's hand. Chest high. Right next to his heart. But Eddie's angle had been bad. He thought he heard Glen say, "Here's payment. Here's

224 Darrell Spencer

what you're after." He thought he saw him pull the trigger. He did hear the sound, like wood cracking, and he saw Glen buckling. Glen crumpled to the ground. Joy tried to scream and didn't. Olive Root dropped the cell phone. Matthew and Mark ran, not to the truck they had come in, but to the back of the house. Noah was right behind them. Eddie knelt by his father. What seemed to be hours later but it was only a short time Eddie looked up and Kefauver and his boys were gone. Eddie could hear sirens coming up Richland Avenue.

Noah kept his Matthew and Mark away from the police. He got them inside the house and upstairs.

Glen hadn't gotten exactly what he wanted. It took him two miserable weeks to die.

In Ohio.

"I never could do that," Cotton said. He was talking about backing up a trailer hitched to a car. Eddie's U-Haul. Eddie had parked in the long driveway off Liar's Corner Road and, when he left, he was going to have to back up so he could get out. Eddie and Cotton were sitting in the butterfly chairs. Eddie here to say good-bye. He had done what he could to sell the house and close things down. Noah and Olive Root would stay on. Sell the businesses.

A.J. would be in Las Vegas by December.

"You do it once, you can do it the rest of your life," Eddie said. "You know how they say it is with riding a bicycle. It's the same. It gets in your bones."

One Mile Past Dangerous Curve   225

"I'd be stuck where I was," Cotton said. "I'd have to unhitch and wrangle the whole thing into going in the right direction."

"Walk up to the trailer," Eddie said, "and act like you're going to push it by hand. Position yourself where you'd need to be to go left or right. Fix that in your head. Then do the same thing from the driver's seat once you get in the car. You get the arc set and it steers itself. Presto."

"That's what they say, but it doesn't work for me."

Eddie said, "You got one axle is all. You're not pushing around some big rig. You're accounting for one axle. Not four. Not six."

"Could be twelve or twenty," Cotton said. "Or one. I'd be grounded."

"Practice will do it."

"And a love of the game."

A.J. came out of the house, and Cotton excused himself.

"My, God, you're beautiful," Eddie said to A.J.

"You too," she said.

Not on Eddie's life. Not Eddie. He had his own number. Average good looks. Personality of a coffee table. But A.J. She made you want to comb your hair and polish your shoes. More to the point, she made you want to think better.

Eddie said, "You're going to have to show your dad how to back up a trailer."

"I don't think so," she said. "You can make it to a hundred years old and never have to use such knowledge."

"You can't think of a situation he might get in?"

"The skill you need to have," she said, "is to avoid such a situation."

"Ah."

She had him. One step ahead of Eddie, one step beyond, one step wiser. Here was the lady who would be moving to Boulder City, Nevada, ten minutes to Lake Mead, an hour to the Strip. Here was the lady who would be meeting M&M. There was a match in the making. Smart on smart.

The door opened and Cotton elbowed his way through. "Rolling Rock," he said.

They drank and didn't talk. Unless you count small stuff. Was Eddie taking 70 across the country? *No.* No? Route 66. *Yeah?* Yeah. *Through Texas?* He had always wanted to see that particular state.

Time got on, and Eddie put himself together to leave.

"One thing," Cotton said.

"You want me here for this?" A.J. said to her father.

He did. He said, "About the murder and the rumor. What if the other woman did it, and the professor was covering up? It's a real possibility. You could argue that he was protecting the lady he loved to the point of going to prison for her."

Love could do that to you.

"We have a saying where I come from," Cotton said. "Goes like this. Except for a slip of the tongue and a change of costume it could have been the other way around."